CROSSINGS 19

Rumore di acque

Noise in the Waters

We dedicate this work to
Mandiaye N'Diaye
coraggio e gioia

Rumore di acque

Noise in the Waters

Marco Martinelli

Edited and Translated from the Italian by

Thomas Simpson

BORDIGHERA PRESS

Library of Congress Control Number: 2013957820

Cover Photo: LUCA BOLOGNESE

2ND PRINTING
October 2014

Printed in the United States.

Published by
BORDIGHERA PRESS
John D. Calandra Italian American Institute
25 West 43rd Street, 17th Floor
New York, NY 10036

CROSSINGS 19
ISBN 978-1-59954-066-5

TABLE OF CONTENTS

ACKNOWLEDGMENTS

The author and translator gratefully acknowledge the online journal *California Italian Studies* for consenting to this republication of the facing page translation that first appeared in their 2011 issue, "Italian Futures" (Vol. 2, Issue 1).

For the United States tour of *Rumore di acque*, Teatro delle Albe wishes most warmly to thank La MaMa Experimental Theatre Club and especially Mia Yoo; Anna Fiore, principal of La Scuola d'Italia Guglielmo Marconi in New York; Montclair State University and especially Teresa Fiore; Professor Edward Muir and the Andrew W. Mellon Distinguished Achievement Award; the Italian Cultural Institutes of Chicago (especially Andrea Raos) and New York; and everyone at Links Hall, Chicago.

Great thanks to Anthony Julian Tamburri, one of three co-editors of Bordighera Press, for making this book possible and for overseeing it editorially.

Special thanks to Glenda Garelli for helping to correct errors in the first edition of this book. Remaining errors are the responsibility of Thomas Simpson.

Super-Special Thanks, from everyone involved in both the U.S. tour and this book, to Silvia Pagliano at Teatro delle Albe for her amazing work and spirit.

Rumore di acque

Noise in the Waters

Marco Martinelli and Teatro delle Albe

Writer and director Marco Martinelli (b. 1956) founded the theatrical cooperative Teatro delle Albe in 1983 together with Ermanna Montanari, Luigi Dadina, and Marcella Nonni. From the beginning, the sharing of duties within the group – conception, composition, production, performance and staging – are such as to speak rather of collective than of individual authorship.

Having already used Romagnol dialect as a vehicle to explore the mythic roots of local and marginal cultures from a global perspective, in 1988 the company expanded their principle of *meticciato teatrale* by working with several Senegalese actors, including Mandiaye N'Diaye, a collaboration that continues to today. One result of this has been *I ventidue infortuni di mor Arlecchino*, a restaging of a *commedia dell'arte* scenario by Carlo Goldoni, in which the traditional mask of Arlecchino becomes an African immigrant. In 1991 the company established the producing organization Ravenna Teatro and in the same year initiated their *non-scuola* project to train young performers. A notable development of the on-going *non-scuola* has been *I Polacchi*, a re-conception of *Ubu Roi*, in which the demonic couple at the center of Jarry's text is surrounded by an army of young *palotini*, who simultaneously conjure and suffer the violence of Mère and Père Ubu. *I Polacchi* has grown into stagings with young actors in Chicago, Naples, Sarajevo, and Diol Kadd, Senegal. The Senegalese production has subsequently been presented in Limôges, Naples and Modena.

Simultaneous to and consistent with their explorations of *meticciato* and their radical engagement with contemporary issues, the company and its members have continued to respond to the classics of the European tradition, as exemplified in the Cantiere Orlando, based on Ariosto's *Orlando furioso*, for the 2000 Venice Biennale, their adaptation of Shakespeare's *Mid-*

summer Night's Dream, and their re-conceptions of works by Molière, including most recently *L'Avare*.

At the same time, through their producing organization Ravenna Teatro and their work at the annual Santarcangelo Festival, the company has become a major motor and organization point for avant-garde theater, linking Eastern and Western Europe, Africa, and the United States. One of the leading contemporary theater cooperatives of Europe, the company and its actors, especially Ermanna Montanari, have received dozens of awards. These awards, a full description of the company's work, and Marco Martinelli's bibliography can be found at the theater company's website: http://www.teatrodellealbe.com.

Rumore di acque in the United States

MARCO MARTINELLI

Now *Rumore di acque* arrives in New York, New Jersey and Chicago, four years after its debut in Ravenna. In New York it comes to La MaMa, forever a symbol of Theater that *doesn't give up*. To put it in black and white terms, we can say there are two ways to do Theater in this world. One is what we call show business. There is another type, though, that combines head and heart, emotion and reason, enchantment and rebellion. A Theater that, following the vision of Augustine of Hippo, an African theologian of the 5th century, embraces the challenge of *Hope*, who is said to have two children: *Scorn* for the way things are, and *Courage* to try to change them. Cheerfully heretical, La MaMa belongs to this second way of doing Theater.

The first story of the sea crossing I heard at Mazara del Vallo, in that part of Sicily that faces Africa, came from a minute, brave Tunisian woman: timid, speaking in broken Italian, she was almost too shy to raise her eyes. I have changed her name to Jasmine and transformed her story while keeping the essentials. It's the first story I heard and the only one, among all those evoked by the General on his volcanic island, that's not about a drowning or a disappearance, about death, but about a life saved. But was she saved? Saved into the talons of the decrepit Italian letcher who boasts that he "never failed to please"? After she spoke, I asked her whether, knowing what she now knows, she would have done it all over again. Her answer was a decisive, "No." She would have stayed in Tunis.

Robert Louis Stevenson often spoke about the "brownies," which he described as "those tiny men who direct the little Theater inside each of us." They're our main collaborators, the ones who construct our nightly "spectacles," the dreams we dream. I'm indebted to the 'brownies' for the character of the General. In my dream, his back is to me, he wants to turn toward me but cannot, he can just barely turn his head, as though he has a crick in his neck. I can't make out who he is. He resembles someone, but who? He's bent over a mass of papers, a pile of sheets covered with badly written numbers, scribbled and scrawled. He looks them over, puts them in order, but the salt water has worn them away; some words are unreadable, some numbers too. Exasperated, he suddenly hurls the papers to the ground. Accounting, bureaucracy as the only way to bear horror. To not think about it. To avoid becoming a carrier of horror.

In rehearsal we thought about Qaddafi and called the character "Qaddafi." We imagined his name as the show's title. We read his speeches, examined his photos. But then.... It was just too simple to blame him, "that guy," that scheming, bloody dictator. It was too easy to strap the mask of guilt onto his face. He is guilty, of course, very guilty; but what about us? And me? Are we innocent? Am I? Can I claim no responsibility for all the tragedies that take place elsewhere, far from my little home? Do I have no responsibility for the death of a brother? Thus we invented that strutting, soliloquizing General, that guard dog alone on a phantom island in the Mediterranean Sea; we constructed him as a *counterfigure*. That embittered, neurotic General, that bureaucrat sick to death of sitting there adding up numbers and dead and listing them in order, that nasty job, every day the same and badly paid on top of it by the chiefs in the capital. That demonic, sarcastic little accountant, that impotent spectator of the massacres on tv news, that guy; he's our *counterfigure*. That monster is us. That's me. The face that finally turns toward me, and in my dream looks straight into my eyes: that's my face.

The General's outburst came gushing out, an unstoppable wave of numbers and images. I wrote it down in snow-covered Mons, Belgium, in the winter of 2010, during off days from rehearsals of our show, *detto Molière*, produced by Daniel Cordova. On Sundays I shut myself up in my room and dived into the Sicilian Channel, the gray sky of Northern Europe turned to

Mediterranean sunlight. I re-read the notes I'd taken during a year of trips to Mazara del Vallo, the most Tunisian city in Europe. We heard stories and testimonies there, but not only stories: we also heard the song of the muezzin on Italian soil. We walked the intricate alleys of the casbah. We saw the brilliant green of the cathedral cupola. And I fed off the strong impressions of my travel companions. Ermanna had immediately *sensed* the presence of an undersea volcano, red water and fire, and out of that she had immediately envisioned a soldier (typical of her, to intuit beyond logical connection well before I dreamt my General). Alessandro filmed everything and picked up bits of Tunisian Arabic from playing soccer with the Tunisian teenagers in our *non-scuola* program; thus he learned to see his family roots in a new light, weaving together genealogy and family legend.

The Mancuso Brothers have enriched this *Oratorio for the Sacrificed* with their voices, powerful as ancient satyrs who seem to cry out the pain of humanity from the depths of an abyss. Since its debut, we have carried this play to many cities in Italy, France, and Germany. The massacre that the General evokes with such deep sarcasm continues as I write today, in October 2013. It is only one of the enormous injustices that strike our planet, and it continues to challenge our claim of innocence. The ongoing slaughter demands that we raise high our Scorn and patiently assert our Courage to bring it to an end. Despite all its limitations, with its nakedness exposed, unseen by the giant mediatic eye, may Theater still nourish our Hope.

Ravenna, October 2013

Translator's Note

THOMAS SIMPSON

Marco Martinelli's *Rumore di acque* was composed, performed and published in 2010. *California Italian Studies* published the play with facing page translation in English in the 2011 issue entitled "Italian Futures" (Vol. 2, Issue 1). The same version was republished, with permission, in *The Mercurian. A Theatrical Translation Review* (Vol. 4, N. 1). The English translation was performed as a staged reading at Victory Gardens Theatre in Chicago as part of the International Voices Project, in 2013. The company brought the play to the US in January and February 2014. At La MaMa Theatre in New York and Montclair State University, New Jersey, it was performed with projected English supertitles, with the actor, Alessandro Renda, speaking some sections in English. For two subsequent performances at Links Hall in Chicago, the play was performed in an experimental version with the English translation integrated into the Italian text.

I am still only scratching the surface of the challenge this text can offer an actor seeking its organic through-line and living rhythm. The play might be even more challenging for an audience than it is for the actor because, as directed by its author, Marco Martinelli, it comes at you so fast and relentless, softened only by the mournful songs of the Mancuso Brothers, that break up the onslaught at key moments, allowing actor and audience to breathe. The headlong pace and unhinged ranting of the speaker assault the pathos inherent in the terrible stories told, a device that frustrates the spectator's wish to settle into a damp warm liberal wallow. The translator is frustrated too, because working line-by-line and section-by-section, you become more aware that each blunt line is nuanced, worded and placed with strategic precision. In place of a method, the translator can only grab on at the beginning and hold on as tight as possible to the onrushing text.

The word "translate" means to bear across, to carry across. To carry *what* across *what*? It must mean to carry something important across a gap. To carry one's body across the sea? The gap between one shore or one language and another is unknowable, uncontrollable, something we cannot see the dimensions of. It can be a matter of space, like the sea, or a matter of incomprehension, as in the gap between one language, one culture, one perception of the world and another. What are we carrying across the gap? It must be something we wish to keep alive, some sort of constant flame, something we want to be able still to recognize once it gets to the other side. But like any voyage, the experience of translation itself necessarily changes that which is carried, if for no other reason than because the relation of the translated thing to its surroundings changes. In practice – which is to say in truth – we can only identify anything as "the same," as itself, by measuring its change, its degree of difference from what it was before. The point is that sameness and difference are inextricably mixed up one with another, and both are illusory. The success or failure of translation, like that of an experience of immigration, can only be measured by its usefulness. How to measure the usefulness of a person translated from her native land into a new one? How to measure the usefulness of a work of theatre translated into a new sphere?

There are at least three translations here, just to start with: first there's the translation of a live performance event into a two-dimensional script, then there's the translation of an Italian text into English, and then there's the translation of a performance event in Italy into a performance event in the United States. This English version is offered only as a jumping-off point for its transformation through the voice and presence of an actor into the eyes, ears, heart and mind of a live audience.

Sparing the reader the obvious excuses, two points of translation call for comment and serve as examples of language difficulties particular to this play:

The title, *Rumore di acque*, epitomizes the deceptive simplicity of the entire text, for *rumore* in this context suggests something more haunting and troubling than mere 'sound', and the plural *acque* similarly evokes something more haunting and remote than the obvious, singular 'water'. The poetic depth of the text's use of water is discussed in Franco Nasi's essay at the end of this volume. The genitive preposition *di* in the title is problematic for its summoning of source, origin, cause and composition. Thus, the English title given here is provisional and feels increasingly unsatisfactory. This is the kind of issue that must be addressed during a rehearsal process, as the text evolves toward a new being in a new setting.

In the section of the play that describes the massacre of seventy-seven immigrants due to the ineptitude of a navy officer, the author writes "*Esse o esse / Esse o esse / Essere o essere*," alluding simultaneously to the the naval distress signal SOS and to a variation on the Italian for Hamlet's "To be or not to be" (in Italian, *essere o non essere*). The Italian homophony of *esse*, the written-out form of the letter s, and the infinitive *essere*, to be, cannot be transferred to English, thus missing Martinelli's bitter play on the difference between Hamlet's choice and the absence of choice for the doomed immigrants. As with everything else here, I appeal to readers for suggestions.

As I write these thoughts I am flying from Chicago to Rome. We use this expression, "to fly." As I soar in a metal tube 30,000 feet in the air toward a welcome in Italy dozens or hundreds of people on the shores of northern Africa are piling onto makeshift boats to entrust their fate to the currents in hopes of reaching Lampedusa or Sicily, thus to escape hunger, war, uselessness. The lucky will survive; many will die at sea. On the other side of the water, Europe needs these people. Europe needs agricultural workers; it needs people to clean, carry, and process its filth. European men need sex workers, it seems. On a different scale, no one can deny that Europe needs change, it needs the new, a future. But by the strange laws of democratic capitalism, and in contrast to me, the African workers who flock to meet Europe's demand must get there illegally, at risk of their lives. It is ironic that a century ago the direction of immigration was reversed: then, Italians went to Africa in search of opportunity. Today, those who make it to Europe sacrifice family and community to wash up on the new shore, naked of identity. Was it so much worse than this on the slave ships? Meanwhile, we who have fallen by sheer chance on the lucky side of this equation find ways to rationalize the atrocious injustice of it, as humans throughout history have rationalized the slavery of others. We fold it into our idea of the normal way of the world, as though it were beyond our control, when in fact we are the cause, the beneficiaries, and the perpetuators. We in the free countries vaunt our tolerance, but it is a shameful sort of tolerance to so easily accept the intolerable as normal. Marco Martinelli's play is about helpless victims of injustice, as seen through the eyes of a soldier in an amorphous, possibly imaginary bureaucratic office, who has been driven insane by the mental contortions required to destroy his natural human empathy, to adapt to horror, to deliberately and consciously not save his brothers and sisters from needless suffering.

Rumore di acque

Noise in the Waters

TEATRO DELLE ALBE

RUMORE DI ACQUE (NOISE IN THE WATERS)
by Marco Martinelli
Devised by Marco Martinelli, Ermanna Montanari
Direction Marco Martinelli

On stage Alessandro Renda

Original live music by Fratelli Mancuso
Space, lights, costume design Ermanna Montanari, Enrico Isola
Costumes by Laura Graziani Alta Moda, A.N.G.E.L.O.
Technical direction Enrico Isola • *Sound engineer* Andrea Villich
Sets by Teatro delle Albe

Technical team
Fabio Ceroni, Luca Fagioli, Danilo Maniscalco, Dennis Masotti

With a contribution from Amir Sharifpour (Opera Ovunque)

Organization and promotion
Marcella Nonni, Silvia Pagliano, Francesca Venturi

With thanks to Tahar Lamri, Gabriele del Grande, Fabrizio Gatti, Francesco Sferlazzo, Antonino Cusumano, Goffredo Fofi, Piera Buscarino, Rosalba Ruggeri, Vincenzo Renda, Marco Carsetti – Associazione Asinitas, Rome, Padre Francesco Fiorino – Fondazione San Vito Onlus di Mazara del Vallo, B.O. Service, W.M. Service

Co-production Ravenna Festival, Teatro delle Albe-Ravenna Teatro, Regione Siciliana, Circuito Epicarmo, Sensi Contemporanei

Under the patronage of
Amnesty International

Rumore di acque was first performed on July 10, 2010, at Teatro Rasi in Ravenna, Italy. The text of *Rumore di acque*, with a note by Marco Martinelli, was published by Editoria & Spettacolo (2010). ISBN: 978-88-89036-93-8. www.editoriaespettacolo.it

E chi ci legge qui?
Non ci si capisce niente
Tutto una confusione
Ma guarda te
Guarda niente
Non c'è niente da guardare
Solo segnacci ovunque
Incomprensibili
Veh, neanche i numeri
Almeno capire i numeri
Così da metterli in ordine
Dai, su
Sforzati almeno di leggere quelli
Se riesci a leggere le cifre
È già un passo avanti
Un numerino dopo l'altro
Ordine
C'è bisogno di ordine
Poi va a finire
Che se la prendono con te
Che non hai lavorato bene
Ecco qui c'è un 1
Son quattro cifre
La prima è un 1
E la terza è sicuramente un 4
Ma la seconda?
Un 2?
Un 6?
O un 8?
La curva in alto è chiara
Ma sotto?
Manca troppo là sotto
Manca
E chissenefrega se manca
Io interpreto

Can anyone read this?
Can anyone make this out?
What a mess
Would you look at this?
Look at what
Nothing to look at
Just scribbles everywhere
Unreadable
Look, not even the numbers
At least make out the numbers
Line them up in order
Come on, let's go
Force yourself at least to read those
If you can make out the figures
It's a step in the right direction
One little digit after another
Order
We need order here
Then it ends up
That it's all your fault
That you did it all wrong
Here we go, this is a 1
Four numbers here
The first is a 1
And the third is a 4 for sure
But the second?
A 2?
A 6?
Or an 8?
This curve above is clear
But underneath?
Too much missing underneath
Missing
Who cares what's missing
I interpret

La scienza è interpretazione
Ricalcolo
Quello è un 2
Niente dubbi
E' un 2
Ricalcolo
Quattro cifre
1
2 appunto
La terza è un 4
Se la quarta è poniamo un 6
O un 7
Un 8
Giusto
L'8 che non era prima
Giusto
E' un 8
Prima era un 2
Il numero intero mi viene
1248
1248
Suona bene
E poi è solo per cominciare
1248
1248
1248
Chi non annega nei primi cento metri
Ha altri cento chilometri per farlo
E se non è la barca che prende acqua
E affonda
È il motore che si rompe
Patatrac
E la manda alla deriva
Per giorni, settimane
Nel buio della notte

Science is interpretation
Recalculate
That's a 2
No doubt
It's a 2
Recalculate
Four digits
1
2 right
The third is a 4
Let's say the fourth is a 6
or a 7
An 8
Right
The missing 8
Right
It's an 8
Before it was a 2
The whole number comes up
1248
1248
Sounds good
A start anyway
1248
1248
1248
If you don't drown in the first hundred meters
You have another hundred kilometers to drown in
And if it's not the boat that takes on water
And sinks
It's the motor breaks down
Patatrac
And you're adrift
For days, weeks
In the dark of night

Ghiaccio e tenebre
Nel sole del meriggio
Arsura
E la merce va a male
1248
1248
Chi può essere
Guarda quest'altro
Facile questo
2
9
1
E poi
E poi un bel 7
Ma sì
2917
Ma sei sicuro che
E' un 7, non c'è dubbio
Questo è un ragazzino
2917
2917
Un nome a caso
Yusuf
Yusuf suona bene
Questo viene dal Sahara Occidentale
Nientemeno
La data non c'è
Cancellata
Che rabbia quando mi si cancellano le date
Yusuf è un ragazzino
Pelle nera
Cosa vuoi che capiscano questi qua
Capiscono niente
Pelle nera
E vai a parlar loro di democrazia

Ice and blackness
Blazing sun
Scorching heat
And the merchandise goes bad
1248
1248
Who could that be
Look at this other
Easy this one
2
9
1
And then
And then a nice 7
Of course
2917
But are you sure that's
A 7, no doubt
This is a kid
2917
2917
Grab a name from the hat
Yusuf
Yusuf sounds good
This kid from Western Sahara
No less
There's no date
Erased
I hate it when the dates fade
Yusuf is a kid
Black skin
What can you expect from these people
They understand nothing
Black skin
And you talk to them about democracy

Ridicolo
Sono ancora sugli alberi
magari si mangiano ancora tra loro
E gli si va parlare di democrazia
Tempo perso
Yusuf
Da poco più di due mesi
Con i pescatori della laguna
La laguna di Naila
Fenicotteri rosa
Pesci e capre nella bassa marea
Una bella cartolina
Qui le acque salate son calme
Ma fuori il mare fa paura
L'Oceano
Yusuf non lo ha mai visto
L'Oceano
Il mare aperto
Sta appena imparando
Guida la barca del padrone
Un due metri nero e blu
Yusuf è uno sbruffone
2917
Sa-tutto-lui
Sempre stato così
Solo perché ha imparato
A mandare avanti la barcuzza del padrone
Si crede chissachi
Comincia a far girar la voce
Per scherzo
Inizia per scherzo
Vi porto io in Europa
In Spagna
Le Canarie sono lì
E che ci vuole

Ridiculous
They're still up in the trees
Still eating each other maybe
And we tell them about democracy
Waste of time
Yusuf
Barely two months
With the fishermen in the lagoon
Naila Lagoon
Pink flamingos
Fish and goats at low tide
Nice postcard
Here the salt waters are calm
But out there the sea is scary
The Ocean
Yusuf's never seen it
The Ocean
The open sea
He's just learning
Drives his boss's boat
Black and blue two meters
Yusuf is a braggart
2917
A know it all
Always been that way
Just because he learned
To pilot his boss's dinghy
Who's he think he is
Word starts going around
As a gag
Starts as a gag
I'll take you to Europe
To Spain
The Canary Islands are just out there
Nothing to it

La barca ce l'ho
Si parte quando si vuole
Mi date la metà
La metà mi basta
Non sono onesto?
La metà esatta
Di quel che vi spillano gli altri
Le Canarie sono lì
Sono Spagna
A un passo
Una notte di viaggio
E che ci vuole
E va a finire
Che quelli ci credono
Cominciano a cercarlo
Yusuuuf!
A portargli i soldi
Yusuuuf!
Non ha mai visto tanti soldi
Tutti assieme
Ma lui non diceva sul serio
Vatti a fidare
Quelli l'han preso sul serio
E gli portano i soldi
Tanti soldi
Lui non li ha mai visti tanti soldi
Tutti assieme
Lui è uno sbruffone
Lui è un so-tutto-io
Lui diceva per ridere
So fare
Ho imparato
Vi porto alle Canarie
Vi porto in Spagna
Barcellona

I got the boat
We'll leave any time
Give me half
Half is enough for me
Don't you trust me?
Exactly half
What the others scam you for
The Canary Islands are just out there
That's Spain
One step away
One night's travel
And what's it take
And it ends up
That they believe it
They seek him out
Yusuuuf!
Money in their hands
Yusuuuf!
Never seen so much cash
All in one place
But he didn't mean it
And you're gonna believe
They thought he meant it
And they bring him money
Lots of money
He's never seen so much cash
All in one place
He's a braggart
He's a know it all
He was only kidding
I know how
I learned
I'll take you to the Canaries
I'll take you to Spain
Barcelona

Real Madrid
Sbruffone
Sa guidare solo il due metri del padrone
Il due metri nero e blu
Nelle acque calme della laguna
Sono in tanti
Gli stanno addosso
Coi soldi nella busta
Lo fissano
Gli occhi come rasoi
Quando si parte
Quando
Stanotte dice Yusuf
E tiene in mano tutti quei soldi
E fa finta di non aver paura
Ma sotto se la fa addosso
E di notte
Scende di corsa le scale del molo
Sbruffone
Yusuf
2917
Ha il fiatone
Dentro!
Tutti su!
Sedici passeggeri
Tutti saharawi
Tutti scesi dall'albero
Cosa vuoi pretendere
Yusuf canticchia
Fa finta di aver coraggio
Gli occhi che ridono
Vi porto alle Canarie
In Spagna vi porto
A vedere il Real Madrid
Il Barcellona

Real Madrid
Braggart
Can barely handle his boss's dinghy
Black and blue two meters
In the calm waters of the lagoon
There's so many of them
They're all over him
Cash in an envelope
They stare at him
Eyes like razors
When do we leave
When
Tonight says Yusuf
And holds all that money in his hand
And pretends he's not afraid
But he's shitting himself
And at night
He runs down the wharf
Braggart
Yusuf
2917
Gasping for breath
All aboard!
Everybody in!
Sixteen passengers
All Saharawi
Barely out of the trees
What do you expect
Yusuf sings
Pretends to be brave
Eyes laughing
I'll take you to the Canaries
To Spain I'll take you
To see Real Madrid
Barcelona

Ha il cuore in gola
Lo sbruffoncello
Accende il motore
Partenza
Stretti stretti
Su quei due metri neri e blu
Neri come la notte
Blu come la paura
Il motore canta a pieni giri
Sulle acque piatte come minerale
Della laguna di Naila
Fenicotteri rosa
Pesci e capre nella bassa marea
Una bella cartolina

(silenzio)

Appena usciti dalla laguna
Un'onda di due metri
Barcuzza piena d'acqua
Annegano tutti
Sprofondano
Anche lo sbruffone
Finito

(silenzio)

In certi punti il mare sa di carne morta

(silenzio)

3999
Se quello è un 9
E quest'altro
3455

Heart in his throat
Little braggart
Yanks the cord
They pull away
Crushed together
Onto those black and blue two meters
Black as night
Blue as fear
Motor hums along full
Water smooth as a diamond
Of the Naila lagoon
Pink flamingos
Fish and goats at low tide
Nice postcard

(silence)

Just outside the lagoon
A two meter wave
Dinghy fills with water
Everyone drowns
Down to the bottom
Even the braggart
All over

(silence)

In some places the sea tastes like dead flesh

(silence)

3999
If that's a 9
And this other one
3455

Mah
E chi ci legge qui?
Non ci si capisce niente
C'è poca luce
in questa baracca di lamiera
C'è poca luce in tutta l'isola
Certo che
Potrebbero far qualcosa
Chiamare un tecnico
Chiamarlo io?
Me la devo sbrigare da solo?
Dovrebbero loro
mettermelo a disposizione
ventiquattrore su ventiquattro
mi fan fare tutto 'sto lavoro
da solo
Ma guarda te
Guarda niente
Non c'è niente da guardare
Solo segnacci ovunque
Incomprensibili
Veh, neanche i numeri
Almeno capire i numeri
Così da metterli in ordine
Dai, su
Sforzati almeno di leggere quelli
Se riesci a leggere le cifre
È già un passo avanti
Un numerino dopo l'altro
Ordine
C'è bisogno di ordine
Poi va a finire
Che se la prendono con te
Che non hai lavorato bene
vogliono la lista come si deve

What?
Can anyone read this?
Can anyone make this out?
So little light
in this sheet metal shack
So little light on this whole island
Sure
They could do something
Call in a technician
Do I call him?
I have to take care of it?
They should
have someone here for me
twentyfour seven
they leave all this work to me
by myself
Would you look at this
Look at what
Nothing to look at
Just scribbles everywhere
Unreadable
Look, not even the numbers
At least make out the numbers
Line them up in order
Come on, let's go
Force yourself at least to read those
If you can make out the figures
It's a step in the right direction
One little digit after another
Order
We need order here
Then it ends up
That it's all your fault
That you did it all wrong
They want the list just so

Ti strigliano
Alzano la voce
E pagano, sì
Ma quando pare a loro
Una miseria
Bravi quelli
bravi
a fare i grossi nei salotti
il caviale, lo champagne
le signorine
ma poi il lavoro sporco
lo lasciano al sottoscritto
Ecco qui c'è un 7
Son quattro cifre
La prima è un 7
E la terza è sicuramente un…
Un 7…
Ma la seconda?
Direi
Ma potrei sbagliare
E' un 7 anche questa?
E pure la quarta è un 7
Troppo facile
7777
Troppo facile
7777
Settanta volte sette
E chissenefrega se è facile
Mica son pagato
Per fare un lavoro difficile
Son pagato e basta
La scienza è interpretazione
Ordine
Se c'è ordine e chiarezza
Tutti col naso all'insù

They rake you over the coals
Raise their voices
And they pay, yeah
But only when they want to
Peanuts
Sharp they are
sharp
play the big shots in their lounges
caviar, champagne
the girls
but the dirty work
they leave to yours truly
Here this is a 7
Four numbers
The first a 7
And the third has got to be a . . .
A 7 . . .
But the second?
I'd say
Could be wrong but
Is this a 7 too?
Even the fourth's a 7
Too easy
7777
Too easy
7777
Seventy times 7
Who cares if it's easy
Not that I'm paid
To do a hard job
I'm paid that's it
Science is interpretation
Order
If there's order and clarity
All with their noses in the air

Tutti rassicurati
A dire che va bene
Che tutto regge
Ordine e chiarezza
Le tabelline
I numeri messi in fila
Per benino

(silenzio)

Però questa è bella
7777
7777
Questo 7777 non mi torna
Qui dentro non c'è un nome solo
Dentro a un numero così
ce ne possono stare settantasette
Te pensa la coincidenza
Settantasette nel 7777
Tutti su un barcone
Ammasso di gambe, braccia, teste
E allora
se sono in settantasette
perché me li mettono su un foglio solo?
Tirano a risparmiare
Settantasette nel 7777
Oppure è mania di simmetria
Sarà
A me non piace la simmetria
Comunque quelli gridano, pregano
nella notte
Gridano e pregano
Quelle cose là
stipati nel barcone
infradiciati

All so secure
It's all going fine
It all holds together
Order and clarity
The charts
Numbers lined up in rows
Just so

(silence)

But this is something
7777
7777
This 7777 doesn't add up
There's not one name only here
Inside a number like this
there could be seventy-seven
What a coincidence
Seventy-seven in 7777
Crammed onto a big boat
Pile of legs, arms, heads
So then
if there's seventy-seven
why'd they give me this one sheet?
Cost-cutting
Seventy-seven on 7777
Or they're nuts for symmetry
Could be
I don't like symmetry
Either way they cry out, they pray
into the night
They cry out and pray
That stuff of theirs
crammed onto the big boat
soaking wet

mangiati da un freddo atroce
schiaffeggiati dalle onde
gridano e pregano
pregano e son presi a schiaffi
una bibbia, un corano
inzuppati nell'acqua
lo stomaco che urla dalla fame
patetici
Arrivano i soccorsi
L'ammiraglio è un italiano
Figlio d'arte
Ammiraglio figlio di ammiragli
Una dinastia
Una garanzia
Una famiglia di ammiragli
Quando chiama il padre al telefono
Sì signor Padre
Sì signor Padre
Stirpe di ammiragli
Sì signor Padre
Manco fosse quello là nei cieli
Sì signor Padre
Al telefono
Chiede consigli
Come si fa signor Padre
In questi casi come si fa
Il barcone pieno di corpi
Ammasso di gambe, braccia, teste
Come si fa
Arrivano i soccorsi
La motovedetta dei militari
quella dell'ammiraglio Signor Figlio
e la nave dei pescatori
quella di Totò
che un pescatore a quei tempi

chewed up by the biting cold
slapped around by the waves
they cry out and pray
pray and get slapped
a bible, a koran
drenched with water
stomach screaming from hunger
pathetic
Here comes the rescue
Admiral's an Italian
Born to the corps
Admiral son of admirals
A dynasty
A guarantee
Whole family of admirals
Calls his father on the phone
Yes Father sir
Yes Father sir
Race of admirals
Yes Father sir
Admiral Who Art in Heaven
Yes Father sir
On the phone
He wants advice
What's done now Father sir
What's done in these cases
Boat loaded with bodies
Pile of legs, arms, heads
What's done now
Here comes the rescue
The military launch
of Admiral Sonny
And the fishing boat
belongs to Totò
fisherman from the old days

se vede gente a mare subito si butta
a quei tempi
Insomma il barcone
la motovedetta
e il peschereccio
tutti e tre in un fazzoletto d'acqua
tre caravelle messe lì dal Destino
il barcone
la motovedetta
e il peschereccio
partono i soccorsi
ognuno fa la sua parte
Poi una manovra sbagliata
Il barcone si spezza in due
E' un classico
E l'ammiraglio figlio di
Invece di spegnere subito le eliche
Che fa?
Che fa?
Non fa
Non spegne subito le eliche
e i settantasette sprofondano
La prima cosa da fare
Quando c'è gente a mare
E' spegnere le eliche
Quello se lo dimentica
Ammiraglio figlio di ammiragli
Sì Signor Padre
Lui se lo dimentica
Tre minuti
In tre minuti
In quei brevi tre minuti
Tutti
Tutti son risucchiati
Fatti a pezzi

sees a man overboard, jumps right in
the old days
Anyway the big boat
the military launch
and the fishing boat
all three in a handkerchief of water
three caravels fated there by Destiny
the boat
the launch
the fishing boat
to the rescue
every man at his post
Then a wrong maneuver
Boat splits in two
Classic
And the admiral's son, son of a
Instead of shutting down the propellers
What's he do?
What's he do?
He doesn't
He doesn't shut down the propellers
and the seventy-seven fall in
First thing to do
Man overboard
Shut down the propellers
But the guy forgets
Admiral son of admirals
Yes Father sir
He forgets
Three minutes
In three minutes
In those three short minutes
Everyone
Everyone sucked in
Sliced to pieces

Massacrati dalle eliche
Triturati dalle eliche
Tutti i settantasette
Bastano tre minuti
Braccia di qua gambe di là
Pastura per i pesci
Mica è colpa loro
Delle eliche intendo
Le eliche non pensano
Le eliche non hanno il cervello
Gli ammiragli dovrebbero
Dico il cervello
Gli ammiragli dovrebbero avercelo
In dotazione
Sciocchezze!
Tuona l'Ammiraglio Padre
Sciocchezze!
Stiam qui a guardare
Sottigliezze
Stupidaggini
E soprattutto silenzio!
Acqua in bocca!
Che nessuno fiati!
Che anno era quello
Quello dei settantasette nel 7777
Ma diavolo
Se mi cancellano pure le date
comunque
erano anni quelli che di esse o esse
ce n'erano anche due o tre al giorno
Esse o esse
Esse o esse
Essere o essere
Alla fine
Non essere

Massacred by the blades
Diced by the blades
All seventy-seven
Only takes three minutes
Arms here legs there
Feast for the fish
Can't blame them
The propellers I mean
Propellers can't think
Propellers have no brain
Admirals should
A brain I mean
Admirals should have one
Standard equipment
Foolishness!
Thunders Admiral Father
Foolishness!
We stand here watching
Fine points
Nonsense!
And above all, silence!
Swallow your words!
Not a breath!
What year was that
The one of the seventy-seven in 7777
But hell
If they erase the dates on me
anyway
in those days SOS
two or three times a day
Save Our Ship
Save Our Souls
To be or to be
In the end
Not to be

Erano anni quelli
ogni giorno due tre barconi
alla deriva
Su ogni barcone
minimo un cadavere
che mica stavi a riportarlo a terra
lo ributtavi a mare
quello era il suo funerale
Non c'è cimitero più efficiente
economico
Un posticino laggiù non costa niente
addobbato come si deve
Ambiente
che dire dell'ambiente
luce e pesci, sabbia e scogli
suggestivo
quello era il suo funerale
Su ogni barcone
minimo un cadavere
Sì Signor Padre
Si Signor Padre
Ho sbagliato Signor Padre
Ma certo Signor Padre
Nessuno lo verrà a sapere
Signor Padre
Agli uomini sarà chiesto il silenzio
Sì Signor Padre
Il silenzio
Fuggire i giornalisti
Fuggire le interviste
Fuggire i ficcanaso
Fuggire le responsabilità
Fuggire le televisioni
Fuggire le tentazioni
Fuggire le commissioni

In those days
every day two three boats
cut adrift
On every big boat
minimum one cadaver
you're not going to tow it to land
toss it back in the sea
there's a funeral for you
No more efficient cemetery than that
economical
cozy little space down there costs nothing
furnished to a t
Atmosphere
consider the atmosphere
light and fish, sand and reefs
evocative
there's a funeral for you
On every boat
minimum one cadaver
Yes Father sir
Yes Father sir
I made a mistake Father sir
Certainly Father sir
No one will know
Father sir
Silence from the crew
Yes Father sir
Silence
Flee the reporters
Flee the interviews
Flee the nosy buggers
Flee responsibility
Flee the television
Flee temptation
Flee the commissions

sì Signor Padre
il silenzio
il silenzio
il silenzio
il silenzio
il silenzio
il silenzio
una bella colata di silenzio

(silenzio)

44
Possibile?
44
Un numero così piccolo
44
ah certo che
con un numero così
si va un po' lontano
parecchio lontano
negli anni
44
Sakinah
44
neanche lei è sola
insieme ad altre trenta
nigeriane
bambine quasi
un carico prezioso
queste facevano vela
queste si muovean per mare
queste andavano per andare
queste le mandavano a fare
di là
sull'altra sponda

Yes Father sir
the silence
the silence
the silence
the silence
the silence
the silence
A cement coating of silence

(silence)

44
Is that possible?
44
such a small number
44
ah, sure
such a number
takes us way back
quite a ways
years ago
44
Sakinah
44
she's not alone either
together with another thirty
Nigerian girls
little girls almost
precious cargo
They went to sea
They took to sail
They rode the waves
They braved the spray
beyond
on the other shore

il mestiere più antico del mondo
un carico prezioso
belle fanciulle
molte di loro già violentate
in mezzo al deserto
usate e abusate
sulla pista degli schiavi
prima i trafficanti
poi i poliziotti di Agadez
poi di nuovo i trafficanti
poi ancora i poliziotti
libici stavolta
alla fine
tutte sul barcone
un barcone già malandato
legno pessimo
un rottame
a occhio lo vedi
che non terrà l'acqua
alla fine
tutte in fondo al mare
Sakinah
Sakinah e le altre trenta
invece che profumate
nei letti dei bianchi
tra le lenzuola di raso
ora giacciono là
nel fondo
smangiucchiate dai pesci
le ossa mutate in corallo
le perle al posto degli occhi

(silenzio)

e il trafficante che canta

world's oldest profession
precious cargo
pretty girls
many already raped
out in the desert
used and abused
on the slave routes
first the traffickers
then the cops in Agadez
then more traffickers
then more cops
Libyan this time
finally
all aboard
boat's a relic
sodden planks
boat's a wreck
just look at it
can't hold water
finally
all of them into the drink
Sakinah
Sakinah and the other thirty
instead of perfume
in white men's beds
between satin sheets
now they lay
on the bottom
fish eaten
of their bones are coral made
those are pearls that were their eyes

(silence)

and the trafficker sings

(silenzio)

Tutti dan la colpa a me
Tutti dan la colpa a me
Ma che colpa ne ho io
Se il tempo era rio

(silenzio)

La barca non ha retto
Il legno era in difetto

(silenzio)

Tutti dan la colpa a me
Tutti dan la colpa a me
Ma che colpa ne ho io
Se il tempo era a schifìo

(silenzio, si guarda attorno)

Oh
Fermi
statevene fermi voi
silenzio
fermi ho detto
Osktù!
Osktù!
Yezzi![1]
Statevene fermi spiriti
Spiriti dei dispersi
Spiriti inabissati
Spiriti liquidi
in poltiglia

(silence)

They all blame me
They all blame me
But the fault ain't mine
If the weather's unkind

(silence)

The boat didn't hold
wood not up to code

(silence)

They all blame me
They all blame me
But it ain't my sin
If the clouds roll in

(silence, he looks around)

. Oh
Hold it
hold it right there you
quiet
hold it I said
Osktù!
Osktù!
Yezzi![2]
Hold still spirits
Spirits of the lost
Spirits in the deep
Liquid spirits
mashed to pulp

che cento, mille volte
avreste preferito una morte asciutta
non muovetevi
qui nessuno si muova
finchè non lo dico io
finchè non ho rimesso tutto in ordine
che quelli là
quelli delle capitali
mi strigliano se non lavoro bene
Certo che la nostra
è una grande politica
su quest'isola li accogliamo tutti
su quest'isola vi accogliamo tutti
spiriti
non respingiamo nessuno
la politica degli accoglimenti
l'ho inventata io
sono il più accorto io
sono il signore dei numeri io
di me si possono fidare
Mi pagano
Quelli delle capitali
Mi pagano il giusto
ogni numero un versamento
in banca
Ordine e chiarezza
Mica per niente ho il petto
gonfio di medaglie
Ordine e chiarezza
Tutti in fila
L'elenco come si deve
Un morto dopo l'altro
La lista aggiornata
E' un lavoraccio
Medaglie o non medaglie

a hundred, thousand times
you'd rather a dry death
don't move
no one moves
until I say so
until I straighten this out
because those guys
those guys in the capital
rake me raw if I screw up
Sure our
policy is grand
on this island all are welcome
on this island you're all welcome
spirits
we refuse no one
open door policy
my own invention
I'm the wisest of all
I'm the lord of numbers
count on me
They pay me
those guys in the capital
Fair pay for honest work
every number a deposit
into my account
Order and clarity
Not for nothing my chest
puffed with medals
Order and clarity
All in a row
Listed just right
One dead body after another
Up-to-date list
Hell of a job
Medals or no medals

Il lavoro sporco tocca a me
A quelli come me
Lasciamo perdere
Inutile lamentarsi
Ti strigliano anche se ti lamenti
Ti fanno il contropelo
I lamentosi son di quella razza
Che vuole vivere con il culo nel burro
Facile per quelli
Sparare sentenze
Ma in mezzo a 'sta marmaglia
Dalla sera alla mattina
Chi ci sta?
Il sottoscritto!
Dove andate?
Spiriti state qua
Osktù!
Osktù!
Restate in fila!
Hayya yallah yallah
Yezzina mel hess
We ennat kil jnun wel afarit
Arkou sci'uyya.
Yezzi![3]
Ve l'ho già detto
Vi accogliamo tutti qui
Nessuno escluso
Non facciamo favoritismi qui
Non avrete da lamentarvi
La politica degli accoglimenti
Questa è la mia isola
qua comando io
sono io il generale
io il presidente
Non muovetevi

I do the dirty work
Guys like me
Forget about it
Useless to complain
They rake the whiners raw
First one way, then back
Whiners are that type
Want to sit their asses in butter
Easy for them
To spew out judgments
But in the middle of this mob
Doing the night shift
Who' always there?
Yours truly!
Where are you going?
Spirits, wait
Osktù!
Osktù!
Stay in line!
Hayya yallah yallah
Yezzina mel hess
We ennat kil jnun wel afarit
Arkou sci'uyya.
Yezzi![4]
I told you
All are welcome
No one refused
No favoritism here
No cause to complain
Open door policy
This is my island
I'm the one in charge
I'm the general
I the president
Don't move

E' un ordine
Anche se il mare ribolle
Lo so
Anche se l'isola trema
Lo so
Colpa del vulcano qua sotto

(silenzio)

Sto perdendo il conto

(silenzio)

Qui
Qui sono tutti morti
sì
ma qualcuno
è più morto degli altri
un affollamento di scintille
vicine e lontane
ce ne sono miliardi
non c'è più differenza di colore
tra il cielo e la terra
nero sopra
nero in basso
un ragazzino
disidratato
emana un odore terribile
nella notte si è svuotato di diarrea
dentro i pantaloni
capita
non bisogna fare gli schizzinosi
capita
mica siamo al club mediterranee
labbra e palpebre secche

That's an order
Even if the sea boils
I know
Even if the island shakes
I know
Fault of this volcano below

(silence)

I'm losing track

(silence)

Here
They're all dead here
yes
but some
are deader than others
a crowd of sparks
near and far
billions of them
all the same color
between heaven and earth
black above
black below
a little boy
dehydrated
gives off such a stink
dumped his diarrhea last night
in his pants
these things happen
no sense being squeamish
these things happen
this ain't Club Med
lips and lids parched

lingua bianca e asciutta
schiacciato là in mezzo
un ammasso di gambe, braccia, teste
e quel ragazzino là in mezzo
una montagna di culi
capita
ingombro di cuori, fegati, budella
non riconosci un proprietario dall'altro
la vita non è proprietà di nessuno
è data a tutti in prestito
come suona vero
che poi cosa vi credevate
quando siete partiti
lo sapevate
lo sapevate, eccome
quando siete partiti all'alba
dal fondo del deserto
quando per sfuggire ai massacri
vi siete intruppati
dentro a quel camion scassato
quel grappolo di bidoni d'acqua
lo sapevate
abbandonati a rincorrere il camion
a piedi nudi
sulla sabbia rovente
il camion che riparte per la Libia
e vi lascia lì
dopo tre giorni senza cibo
inginocchiati
a ricevere le frustate
i colpi dei militari
tubi di gomma
cavi elettrici
lo sapevate
fammi un regalo

tongue white and dry
crushed in between
a mass of legs, arms, heads
and that little boy in the middle
mountain of asses
these things happen
load of hearts, livers, guts
can't tell who they belong to
life belongs to no one
it's on loan to all of us
how true that sounds
anyway what'd you think
when you set out
you knew
you knew, for sure
when you set out at dawn
from deep in the desert
when to escape the massacres
you herded into
that broken old truck
with a handful of water tanks
you knew
running full out after the truck
barefoot
on the scalding sand
truck heading for Libya
leaves you there
three days no food
on your knees
to be whipped
the soldier's blows
rubber tubes
electric cables
you knew
gimme a present

gridano i militari
fammi un regalo, su
oh ma questi son testardi
niente vogliono regalarci
e giù frustate
su, diecimila franchi
cosa vuoi che sia
diecimila franchi
quando sarai in Europa
li guadagnerai in due ore
lo sapevate
e i militari ridono
e i militari sfottono
noi già pregavamo Dio
che voi ancora suonavate i tam tam
e vi mangiavate come animali
ridono i militari
e vi trascinano
nella baracca delle torture
tubi di gomma e cavi elettrici
qualcuno paga
qualcuno no
qualcuno telefona a casa
ci vogliono altri soldi
altri soldi vi scongiuro
ma come
ma per chi
siamo nella miseria
in mezzo alle bombe
e tu ci chiedi ancora soldi?
Te li abbiamo già dati
te ne abbiamo già dati un mucchio
alla partenza
ci siamo indebitati fino al collo
e non ti son bastati?

the soldiers scream
gimme a present, come on
my they're stubborn
where's our presents
blows rain down
come on, ten thousand francs
that's nothing
ten thousand francs
when you get to Europe
you'll make that in two hours
you knew
and the soldiers laugh
and the soldiers mock
we were already praying to God
while you were still beating drums
and eating each other like animals
the soldiers laugh
and they drag you
to the torture room
rubber tubes and electric cable
some pay
some don't
some phone home
they want more money
more money I beg you
but how
but for who
we don't have it
they're bombing us
and you want more money?
We already gave you
we gave you so much
when you set out
in debt up to our necks
that's not enough for you?

Non dovresti già essere in Francia
a quest'ora?
In Italia?
In Svezia?
lo sapevate
abbandonati nel deserto
a cuocere vivi
a impazzire sotto il sole
a dimenticare anche il vostro nome
lo sapevate
che nessuno vi avrebbe tirato fuori
né padre
né madre
né fratello
né Stato
nessun governo alzerà la bandiera
nessun cristiano piangerà la vostra
sorte
morte
lo sapevate
figli di un cane
figli di nessuno
e allora?

(silenzio)

6 e poi?
E poi 5
E poi?
6 e 5 e poi
ancora 5
e poi?
E poi mi stai antipatico
6 e poi 5 e ancora 5
mi stai antipatico

Shouldn't you be in France already
by now?
In Italy?
In Sweden?
you knew
abandoned in the desert
to roast alive
going mad in the sun
forgetting your own name
you knew
that no one could get you out
neither father
nor mother
nor brother
nor State
no country will raise the flag
no Christian will weep over your
wasted breath
empty death
you knew
sons of bitches
sons of nobodies
what d'you expect?

(silence)

6 and what?
And then 5
And then?
6 and 5 and then
another 5
and then?
And then I don't like you
6 and then 5 and another 5
I don't like you

lasciamo perdere
passiamo a un altro
oh, questo sì
questo sì che si legge
1 e poi
e poi niente
sembra che lo fanno apposta
l'acqua
la salsedine
le carte
i numeri si cancellano
e tocca a quelli come me
hai voglia di protestare
il petto gonfio di patacche
e invece tocca a me
a quelli come me
sgobbare
qua sotto
al buio
che perdo il conto
ricomincia, su
ricalcolo
ero sull'1
ho capito ma poi
ricalcolo
poi c'è un altro 1
e un altro 1
e un altro 1
sta a vedere che come prima
tutti quei 7
adesso
1111
1111
possibile
possibile che vengano fuori

leave it
move on to the next
oh yeah, this one
this one you can read
1 and then
and then nothing
It's like they do it on purpose
the water
the salt
the papers
the numbers fade
then it's up to those like me
I should protest
chest puffed with medals
but it's up to me
and others like me
slaving away
down here
in the dark
I lose track
come on, start over
recalculate
I was on 1
I get that but then
recalculate
then there's another 1
and another 1
and another 1
how about that, before
it was all 7s
now
1111
1111
is it possible
is it possible that such

numeri così raggianti
in questa oscurità
1111
a me non piace la simmetria
1111
Jasmine
da Tunisi
dalla casbah
su per il canale di Sicilia
1111
Jasmine
a ottocento metri dalla riva
patatrac
la barcaccia si spezza
Jasmine impavida
li fa a nuoto quegli ottocento metri
tirandosi dietro l'amica
a nuoto se la tira dietro
ma no che non ce la fa
l'amica ha le gambe spezzate
un corpaccione
uno scatolone di donna
1111 invece
testarda
Jasmine
forzuta e piccolina
se la porta dietro
come un valigione di grasso
quella sua amica
gli ultimi ottocento a nuoto
non finiscono mai
alla fine ce la fa
la Sicilia
la Sicilia encantada
la mettono a lavorare

blazing numbers shine
in this darkness
1111
I don't like symmetry
1111
Jasmine
from Tunis
from the casbah
crossing the channel up to Sicily
1111
Jasmine
eight hundred meters from shore
patatrac
the wreck of a boat splinters
Jasmine fearless
she swims those eight hundred meters
towing her friend behind her
swims and tows her friend
but no, she can't make it
friend's legs are broken
big fat body
big square box of a woman
but 1111
stubborn
Jasmine
little and strong
tows her friend behind
like a big suitcase of fat
that friend of hers
swims that last eight hundred
it never ends
but she makes it
Sicily
Sicily encantada
they put her to work

non perdono tempo quelli
quelli che l'han portata lì
fidati, Jasmine
la mettono a sgobbare
dall'alba al tramontare
da un ottantenne
nella casetta di un ottantenne
nella villetta di un ottantenne
la serva, fa
fa un po' di tutto
la serva serve
1111
Jasmine lo serve l'ottantenne
anche per quella cosa là
perchè
chi può sostenere
che a ottantanni non si sia in grado
anche quella cosa là
1111
a Jasmine non piace
a chi piace?
ma lei la fa
pensa a quegli altri
smangiucchiati dai pesci
e la fa quella cosa là
anche con l'ottantenne
pensa giorno e notte
ai parenti a casa
che aspettano
aspettano da lei
aspettano che lei
Jasmine la fa
anche con l'ottantenne
lui
non si crede male

they don't waste time there
the ones who sent her there
trust us Jasmine
she starts slaving
dawn to dusk
eighty year old man
little house of an eighty year old
little bungalow of an eighty year old
works like a slave
does a little of everything
the servant serves
1111
Jasmine serves the eighty year old
does that too
because
who can say
that just because someone's eighty
he can't do that too
1111
Jasmine doesn't like it
who would?
but she does it
thinks about the others
gnawed at by the fish
and so she does that too
with the eighty year old
thinks night and day
about her folks back home
waiting
waiting on her
waiting for her
Jasmine does it
with the eighty year old too
he
thinks he's good stuff

dice che è sempre piaciuto lui
che mai ha avuto problemi lui
con le femmine

(silenzio)

paga
lui
paaaagaaaaaa

(silenzio)

12345
non identificato
12876
non identificato
14545
non identificato
26
accidenti
non identificato
ma un numero così
se fossi un collezionista
varrebbe oro
3462
non identificato
4359
non identificato
6758
non identificato
4445
non identificato
789
non identificato
3989

says he never failed to please
never had any problems
with the skirts

(silence)

he pays
he
paaaayyyys

(silence)

12345
unknown
12876
unknown
14545
unknown
26
damn
unknown
but a number like that
if I were a collector
would be pure gold
3462
unknown
4359
unknown
6758
unknown
4445
unknown
789
unknown
3989

non identificato
1290
non identificato
15677
non identificato
23591
possibile?
Un numero così alto
forse c'è un errore
comunque
non identificato
2487
non identificato
2488
non identificato
2489
non identificato
sabbia nericcia
fumo e bitume
qua sotto il vulcano lavora
altro se lavora
2490
non identificato
2491
non identificato
2492
non identificato
2493
non identificato
Scirocco senza vento
fa squagliare anche le pietre
2494
non identificato
2495
non identificato

unknown
1290
unknown
15677
unknown
23591
is that possible?
that's too high
maybe an error
either way
unknown
2487
unknown
2488
unknown
2489
unknown
blackish sand
smoke and bitumen
here below the volcano works
damn if it doesn't
2490
unknown
2491
unknown
2492
unknown
2493
unknown
Desert heat no wind
melts even the rocks
2494
unknown
2495
unknown

2496
non identificato
2497
non identificato
lapilli e spruzzi sulfurei
schegge e lava incendiaria
il cratere di ceneraccio
e fango scuro
e chi ci vede con tutto 'sto fumo
Tunisi sarà laggiù
sarà laggiù?
dall'altra parte c'è Malta
in mezzo Lampedusa
l'isola dei Conigli
ma chi le vede adesso
chi le vede
lapilli e spruzzi sulfurei
dentro gli occhi
schegge e lava incendiaria
giù nella gola
certi giorni non mi ci raccapezzo
brucio dalla testa ai piedi
perdo le coordinate
3389
non identificato
569
non identificato
16781
non identificato
6546
non identificato
6743
non identificato
7122
non identificato

2496
unknown
2497
unknown
spitting stones and sulfur
shards and flaming lava
crater of lye ash
and dark mud
and who can see with all this smoke
Tunis must be down there
is it down there?
Malta on the other side
Lampedusa in the middle
Rabbit Island
but who can see them now
who can see them
spitting stones and sulfur
in my eyes
shards and flaming lava
down my throat
some days I don't know which way's up
I burn from head to toe
I lose my bearings
3389
unknown
569
unknown
16781
unknown
6546
unknown
6743
unknown
7122
unknown

1681
non identificato
1601
non identificato
luce rossa
non identificato
acqua verdognola
non identificato
tremolìo e vomito
non identificato
ricoperto dalle alghe
fino alla coscia
fino al ginocchio spappolato
non identificato
ripescato qualche giorno dopo
faccia irriconoscibile
faccia divorata dai pesci
non identificato

(silenzio)

certo che i pesci son delinquenti
non guardano in faccia a nessuno

(silenzio)

Maledetti squali
maledetti pescecani
maledette triglie
e tonni
e leviatani
e bahamuth
e orche
e zaratani
maledetti sampietrini

1681
unknown
1601
unknown
red light
unknown
greenish water
unknown
trembling and vomit
unknown
coated with algae
up to the thigh
kneecap gnawed away
unknown
fished out days later
face unrecognizable
fish-eaten face
unknown

(silence)

no respect for the law, these fish
no respect for anyone

(silence)

Damn sharks
damn barracuda
damn mullet
and tuna
and leviathans
and bahamut
and killer whales
and giant turtles
damn John Dorys

maledetti pesci palla
maledetti pesci spada
e martello
e tigre
e coltello
maledetti pesci lupo
iene dalla bocca larga
maledetti voi
sciacalli e sciacalletti degli abissi
voi
belve del mare
mandrie così assatanate
che non fate differenza
tra questo e quello
non fate differenza
e con le larghe mascelle spalancate
tirate morsi
a tutto quel ben di dio
che vi capita intorno
a pacchi ve li trangugiate
quei cadaveri
quei corpicini senza più luce
maledetti voi
che impedite a me
ammè
di fare il mio lavoro
di metterli in fila
di dargli un nome
a quei trapassati inquieti
che non stan fermi un secondo
mi riempiono l'isola di strida
maledette voi
creature delle acque
ve la meritate questa predica
altro se ve la meritate

damn blowfish
damn swordfish
and hammerheads
and tigerfish
and cutlassfish
damn seawolves
wide mouth hyenas
damn you all
jackals and jackalettes of the deep
you
beasts of the sea
roaming in demonic packs
no difference to you
between one thing and another
no difference to you
those jaws gaping wide
bite off chunks
of all that bounty
pouring down from above
in packs you gobble down
those cadavers
those little lightless bodies
damn you
you keep me
me
from doing my work
of lining them up
of giving a name
to those restless departed
they won't stay still a second
they fill my island with screams
damn you
creatures of the sea
you deserve this sermon
you deserve lots worse

vi ingozzate di tutto
non fate differenza tra polpa e polpa
tutto buttate giù
in questo mare di mezzo
chi vi credete?
I becchini ufficiali?
I becchini dell'impero?
Chi vi ha autorizzato?
E prima fatemeli contare, no?
Delinquenti
delinquenti organizzati
ve la meritate questa predica
ho il sangue avvelenato
ho il fegato grosso
non si mettono i bastoni tra le ruote
a un sorvegliante integerrimo
a un funzionario solerte come me
eh no, così non si fa
non sta bene
perchè non distinguete
tra numero e numero?
Perché non siete più precisi?
Cos'è tutta 'sta confusione?
'Sto magna magna?
E d'altronde
A ben guardarvi
non avete testa!
La testa, dico
Voi non ce l'avete
Un collo
che ve la distingua dal corpo
Voi non ce l'avete
E quindi
Cosa si può pretendere alla fin fine
Da gente come voi?

you suck it all down
you can't tell flesh from flesh
you cram it all in
in this middle sea
who do you think you are?
The official gravediggers?
The gravediggers of empire?
Who appointed you?
At least let me count them first, hey?
Criminals
organized criminals
you deserve this sermon
you poison my blood
you burst my liver
you don't sabotage
a superhonest supervisor
a hard worker like me
nope, it's not fair
it's not right
can't you tell
one number from another?
Can't you be more exact?
What's all this chaos?
This all-you-can eat?
Anyway
look at you
you have no head!
A head, I'm saying
You don't have one
No neck
to set your head off from your body
You don't have one
And so
What can we expect after all
from such as you?

Come vi devo parlare,
squali?
Devo gridare?
Fare come il Tonitruànte
Governatore e motor del cielo
Imitarne il vocione?
Cosa devo strologare
per aprirvi le orecchie
quelle orecchie da pesci che neanche avete
sturarvi il cerume che ve le sbarra
perchè proviate un po' di pena
per me in primis
ma anche
toh
per quella pazzerella
per quello scheletrino tra le rocce
la 6132
Obedience la posso chiamare
bel nome
Obedience
scappata dalla guerra e dalle bombe
Obedience
chiamiamola così
che obbediente ha seguito il suo destino
e che doveva fare
che scelta aveva
libero arbitrio direte voi
il questurino dei Fati dico io
ha deciso di scappare
un giorno qualunque
impugnare l'alba come un coltello
e fuggire
fuggire la sua patria incerta
la terra natìa
e le torture certe

How can I talk to you,
sharks?
Do I have to yell?
Thunder down like Jupiter
Governor and driver of the stars
Come on with the big voice?
What hocus pocus
Will ever open your ears
do you fish even have ears?
scrape out the wax that clogs them
so you feel some pity
for me in primis
but also
come on
for that silly little girl
for that little skeleton on the rocks
number 6132
Obedience I'll call her
pretty name
Obedience
fled from war and bombs
Obedience
let's call her
who obediently followed her destiny
what else could she do
what choice did she have
you talk about free will
the beat cop of Fate I'd say
she decided to escape
one day just like the others
seize dawn in her fist like a knife
and flee
flee her uncertain homeland
her native land
and certain torture

per farsi sbucanare prima
dai soliti militari infoiati
dai trafficanti
e poi
perduta negli abissi
farsi spolpare da voi
squali!
Per essere ospite
una delle tante
al vostro banchetto!
Maledetti ingordi!
Bella conclusione
Obedience
obbediente al Fato
obbediente al vostro stomaco
che non si sazia mai!
Squali!
Porci del mare!
Che tutto divorate
sfigurate
e non vi basta mai!
Siate un po' più umani,
squali!

(silenzio)

E Jean-Baptiste?

(silenzio)

E Jean-Baptiste?

(silenzio)

Jean-Baptiste

only to get punctured
by the usual horny soldiers
then the traffickers
and then
lost in the deep
get her flesh torn away by you
sharks!
To be a guest
one of the many
at your banquet!
Damned gluttons!
Nice conclusion
Obedience
obedient to Fate
obedient to your gut
that never gets enough!
Sharks!
Pigs of the sea!
You devour everything
disfigure everything
and it's never enough for you!
Be a little more humane,
sharks!

(silence)

And Jean-Baptiste?

(silence)

And Jean-Baptiste?

(silence)

Jean-Baptiste

è un pischello
poco più che un bimbo
in mezzo a tutti gli altri
il gommone alla deriva
da cinque giorni alla deriva
ne teneva dodici
son partiti in quaranta
ma il motore
patatrac
e allora alla deriva
sballottati sul gommone
Jean-Baptiste guarda i più grandi
qualcuno ha gli occhi spenti
vuole dormire
come si fa a dormire
non dovete dormire
con l'acqua che ci arriva
all'ombelico
non si deve dormire
Jean-Baptiste resisti
ma se non resistono loro
che facevano i grossi
alla partenza
solo acqua tutto attorno
l'orizzonte
il cielo
sembrano anche loro d'acqua
niente più da mangiare
niente più da bere
sei in mezzo a tutta quell'acqua
e non puoi berne una goccia
le onde cominciano
trascinano i più deboli nel fondo
Jean-Baptiste no
Jean-Baptiste è poco più che un bimbo

is a sprout
hardly more than a baby
in with all the others
rubber raft adrift
five days adrift
it holds twelve
forty piled in
but the motor
patatrac
so they're adrift
tossing on the rubber raft
Jean-Baptiste watches the grownups
One with eyes extinguished
he wants to sleep
how can you sleep
better not sleep
with water up to
your belly button
better not sleep
Jean-Baptiste stay awake
but if the grownups can't
who were so bossy
at the start
nothing but water everywhere
the horizon
the sky
seem made of water too
nothing left to eat
nothing left to drink
water water everywhere
not a drop to drink
the waves rise up
drag the weakest down
Jean-Baptiste no
Jean-Baptiste is hardly more than a baby

ma è forte
la mamma lo ha riempito di gri gri
e lui ora se li divora
ce n'è uno apposta per non annegare
fatto di sabbia e di ossicini
di formule magiche
se lo mangi non annegherai
stai sicuro
poi ne ha un altro
che serve a diventare invisibili
a cosa gli serve adesso
a niente
quello avrebbe dovuto usarlo
nel campo da calcio
nel campo da calcio del villaggio
là sì
diventare invisibile
e far impazzire gli avversari
fargli lo sgambetto
rubargli il pallone tra le gambe
e passarlo ai suoi
a cosa gli serve adesso
il gri gri per diventare invisibile
il gommone alla deriva
non dormite, non dormite
se dormite è peggio
tengono gli occhi spalancati
fuori dalle orbite
schizzati
che cosa vedono
quei cerchi bianchi
che cosa vedono
vedono torri e città fantasma
vedono minareti e palazzi
vedono fate e sirene

but strong
mama filled him with gri gri
and now he devours them
one protects from drowning
made of sand and little bones
magic spells
if you eat it you'll never drown
you're safe
he's got another
that'll make him invisible
what use is it now
none
he should have used it
on the soccer field
on the soccer field in the village
there, yes
become invisible
drive your opponents crazy
trip them up
steal the ball from between their legs
pass it to your team
but what use is it now
gri gri for invisibility
rubber raft drifting
don't sleep, don't sleep
worse if you sleep
eyes wide open
bulging from their sockets
bugged out
what do they see
those white circles
what do they see
they see phantom towers and cities
they see minarets and palaces
they see fairies and mermaids

vedono i soccorritori che non soccorrono
non ci sono
vedono e stravedono
la morte no
quella non la vedono quella
li ha già afferrati per il collo
e se li trascina giù come un braccio armato
Jean-Baptiste
Jean-Baptiste
è partito anche se la madre
non voleva
ah no
non voleva
solo questo figlio mi è rimasto
questo non lo posso perdere
lo scafista
l'aveva rassicurata
stai tranquilla
con me tuo figlio è già di là
è già in Europa che lavora
e ti telefona tutte le sere
stai tranquilla
lo scafista
che ha messo in moto il gommone
e dopo trecento metri si è buttato
è ritornato a nuoto
e dopo poco era già là
a bersi una birra coi soci
all'asciutto
stai tranquilla
lui è tornato a nuoto
e li ha lasciati là a bisticciare
chi lo guida il gommone
i grandi che fanno i grossi
lo guido io

they see rescuers who don't rescue
they aren't there
they see and deep see
death no
that they can't see
it already has them by the neck
and drags them down with an iron fist
Jean-Baptiste
Jean Baptiste
he left although his mother
was against it
ah no
was against it
the only son I have left
I can't lose this one
the trafficker
reassured her
don't worry
with me your boy's already on the other side
already in Europe with a job
he calls you every night
don't worry
the trafficker
who started the motor running
and after three hundred meters jumped
and swam back to shore
in no time was back
having a beer with his pals
nice and dry
don't worry
he swam back
and left them there to quarrel
who's guiding this raft
the grownups start shouting
I'll pilot

no, lo guido io
tutti che vogliono comandare
lo scafista
stai tranquilla
trecento metri
e poi è tornato a nuoto
Jean-Baptiste tace
troppo piccolo
che ci pensino i grandi
e i grandi ci pensano
ma sono tutti impauriti
quelli il mare non l'han mai visto
quelli son tutti contadini
vai di qua
gira di là
le stelle
non le sai leggere le stelle
vai dritto incapace
incapace a me?
Quasi le mani addosso
tre giorni passati a girare
attorno allo stesso punto
fin quando il motore si è rotto
quattro, cinque giorni alla deriva
sei, sette, otto giorni alla deriva
Jean-Baptiste non impazzire
pensa a tua madre
quando sarai di là
la chiamerai tutte le sere
sto bene, mamma
lavoro
i soldi qua si trovano per strada
non ti bastano
quelli che ti ho mandato ieri
te ne manderò altri

no, I'll pilot
everyone's the boss
the trafficker
don't worry
three hundred meters
then he swam back
Jean-Baptiste keeps quiet
too little
leave it to the grownups
let the grownups handle it
but they're all afraid
no one's ever seen the sea
bunch of farmers
go this way
turn that way
the stars
can't you read the stars
go straight you fool
you call me a fool?
Almost a fistfight
three days circling
around the same point
until the motor died
four, five days adrift
six, seven, eight days adrift
Jean Baptiste don't lose your mind
think of mama
when you get there
you'll call her every night
I'm fine, mama
I have a job
money grows on trees here
if what I sent yesterday
isn't enough
I'll send you more

Jean-Baptiste resisti
non ti addormentare
non chiudere gli occhi
prega Jean-Baptiste
prega
io questo gri gri me lo conservo
sabbia e conchiglie
questo è fatto apposta
questo mi servirà davanti alla polizia
metti che mi sparano addosso
sabbia e conchiglie mi proteggeranno
devieranno i colpi
Jean-Baptiste non cedere
è un bambino, poco più
ma è forte
il gommone è alla deriva
c'è confusione là sopra
tutti quei grandi come donnicciole
chi piange
chi grida
chi vomita
qualcuno va fuori di testa
vede la terra
terra!
terra!
e si butta
solo un miraggio
il mare lo inghiotte
Jean-Baptiste
non far lo scemo
tu non ti buttare
lì dentro devi stare
il gommone è la salvezza
il gommone ti porterà di là
il gommone

Jean-Baptiste stay awake
don't fall asleep
don't close your eyes
Jean-Baptiste pray
pray
I'll set this gri gri aside
sand and shells
this one special
for when the police come
say they're shooting at me
sand and shells will protect me
turn away the shots
Jean-Baptiste don't give in
he's a baby, little more
but strong
raft adrift
noise up front
all those grownups like old women
some weeping
some screaming
some vomiting
one's out of his head
he sees land
land!
land!
and jumps in
only a mirage
sea swallows him
Jean Baptiste
don't be stupid
don't jump in
stay there inside
the raft is salvation
the raft will get you there
the raft

anche se adesso gira su se stesso
il gommone
è il guscio che ti protegge
il gommone è come un gri gri
accanto a Jean-Baptiste
c'è uno dei grandi
uno di quelli
che litigavano alla partenza
abbandonati dallo scafista
uno che gridava forte
più forte degli altri
so io come guidarlo 'sto coso
se non mi date retta
vi spacco la testa
adesso è la sua testa che penzola
Jean-Baptiste lo chiama
grida il suo nome
prova a smuoverlo
gli occhi spalancati
quello non batte ciglio
la testa a pelo d'acqua
penzola come cosa morta

(silenzio)

Nubi che oscurano il cielo
stanotte non ci sono stelle
nero sopra
nero in basso
A un tratto
Jean-Baptiste si alza in piedi
dice, sicuro
io torno da mia madre
e si tuffa

although now it's spinning
the raft
is the shell protecting you
the raft is like a gri gri
next to Jean-Baptiste
is one of those grownups
one of the ones
who was arguing at the start
abandoned by the trafficker
one who yelled the loudest
louder than the others
I know how to run this thing
if you don't listen to me
I'll crack your head open
now his head's lolling
Jean-Baptiste calls him
yells his name
tries to budge him
eyes bugged out
that one doesn't blink
head brushes the water
hangs like a dead thing

(silence)

Clouds cover the sky
no stars tonight
black above
black below
All at once
Jean-Baptiste stands up
sure of himself
I'm going home to mama
jumps in

(silenzio)

Nuota per un po'
quanti metri
venti?
trenta?
e poi viene tirato giù
scompare

(silenzio)

scompare

(silenzio)

E' vero che a volte
mi invitano
alle loro feste
mi sorridono
mi fanno sentire importante
generale Lei
non mi chiami generale
presidente Lei
non mi chiami presidente
ma come cazzo vuol esser chiamato
e va bene
vada per presidente
su
riprenda col panegirico
e quello riprende
presidente Lei
è un simbolo di libertà
presidente Lei
è un modello per le nuove generazioni
presidente Lei

(silence)

He swims a little
how far
twenty meters?
thirty?
then gets pulled down
disappears

(silence)

disappears

(silence)

True, sometimes
they invite me
to their parties
they smile
make me feel important
Mr. General
oh, don't call me General
Mr. President
oh, don't call me President
so what the fuck should I call you
okay then
let's go with President
hup
again with the panegyric
so he starts again
Mr. President, you
you are a symbol of liberty
Mr. President, you
are a model for the younger generation
Mr. President

la sua politica degli accoglimenti
mi sorridono
mi intervistano
mi fanno sentire utile
sono tutti amici
anche quelli che prima
voltavano la testa
dall'altra parte
anche quelli che un tempo
fingevano di non conoscermi
anche quelli
quando è il momento
anche quelli mi cercano
fanno affari col sottoscritto
mi strizzano l'occhietto
anche quelli
non si tirano indietro
quando è il momento
senza la Sua politica
presidente
i nostri governi faticherebbero
e te credo
grazie alla Sua politica
presidente
le nostre democrazie rifiatano
e te credo
per questo Le siamo riconoscenti
grazie
prego
i nostri accordi bilaterali
presidente
illuminano il mondo
mi offrono lo champagne
il caviale
scattiamo le foto insieme

your open door policy
they smile at me
they interview me
they make me feel useful
they're all friends
even the ones who used to
turn their heads
away
even the ones who used to
pretend not to know me
even them
when the moment comes
even they seek me out
they make deals with yours truly
they give me the wink
even them
they're not shy
when the moment comes
without your program
President
our administration would suffer
believe you me
thanks to your program
President
our democracy thrives
believe you me
we are so grateful to you
thank you
you're welcome
our bilateral accords
President
enlighten the world
they offer me champagne
caviar
we take group pictures

siamo gente di mondo
Roma
Berlino
Mosca
Parigi
Tri-po-lì
ci incontriamo regolarmente
sappiamo sorridere
rispondere ai giornalisti
anche ai rompicoglioni
fare le battute
al momento giusto
usare le parole chiave
libertà!
progresso!
felicità dei popoli!
fanculo i popoli
convivenza civile!
fanculo la convivenza civile
crociere per tutti!
fanculo le...
no...
non fanculo le crociere
anzi
viva
viva le crociere
un settore che non conosce crisi
quelli che vanno in crociera
aumentano giorno dopo giorno
è un'epidemia
un tempo era roba da ricchi
come il tennis
oggi è un passatempo popolare
turismo di massa
ne vedo passare tre al giorno

we are men of the world
Rome
Berlin
Moscow
Paris
Tri-po-lì
we have regular meetings
we know how to smile
answer the reporters
even the ballbreakers
kid around with them
at the right moment
toss in the key words
freedom!
progress!
the people's happiness!
fuck the people
shared community!
fuck the shared community!
cruises for all!
fuck the. . .
no. . .
don't fuck the cruises
on the contrary
long live
long live the cruise ships
a sector that knows no recession
the cruise shippers
grow by the day
it's an epidemic
used to be for the rich
like tennis
now it's for everyone
mass tourism
I watch three go by a day

di navi da crociera
li sento divertirsi
là sopra
ballano e se la spassano
allegria!
baldoria!
là sopra fan di tutto
è lì il segreto
certo che mi pagano poco
mi pagano
non dico di no
ma troppo poco
una miseria
se paragonato al lavoro che faccio
su questo schifo di isola
mica c'è luce qua sotto
un fetore
colpa del vulcano
lavoro sporco, ripeto
accogliere e contare
contare e accogliere
tenere la lista aggiornata
un lavoraccio
vaglielo a spiegare
al Ministro dell'Inferno
lui la fa facile
il Ministro dell'Inferno
lui alza la voce
il Ministro dell'Inferno
è più facile accogliere che respingere
è più facile accogliere che respingere?
non è mica vero
è falso
non c'è niente di più falso
signor Ministro

cruise ships
I hear them having fun
up there
they dance and party
let's have fun!
let's go wild!
they do it all up there
that's the secret
sure, they don't pay me much
they pay me
I don't say they don't
but too little
peanuts
considering the work I do
on this wretched island
no light down here
the stench
because of the volcano
dirty work, I repeat
collect and count
count and collect
keep the list up to date
nasty work
try to explain it
to the Secretary of the Inferno
easy job for him
the Secretary of the Inferno
he raises his voice
the Secretary of the Inferno
It is easier to accept than reject
Is it easier to accept than reject?
That's not true
it's false
nothing more false than that
Mister Secretary sir

solo una carogna
può mettere in giro una voce simile
da quanto tempo sono alle sue dipendenze
signor Ministro?
da quanto tempo sgobbo come uno schiavo?
tenere la lista aggiornata
degli annegati
le sembra cosa da poco
signor Ministro?
Le sembra cosa da poco
questa montagna di morti
che si alza immacolata verso il cielo
le sembra cosa da poco?
La vede Lei la cima
signor Ministro?
La vede?
E poi tenerli tutti qua
ammassati
che ancora non ho capito
come facciamo a starci tutti
su questo sputo di terra
su questo francobollo
Jean-Baptiste per esempio
si alza in piedi, sicuro
io torno da mia madre
si tuffa
scompare
che numero è Jean-Baptiste
a che numero mi corrisponde
signor Ministro
io non lo so
io, generale e presidente
incaricato del censimento
io non lo so
che numero è Jean-Baptiste

only a bastard
could spread that idea
how long have I worked for you
Mister Secretary sir?
how long have I labored like a slave?
keep the list up to date
of the drowned
Does it seem so little to you
Mister Secretary sir?
Does it seem so little
this mountain of dead
that rises immaculate to the sky
does it seem so little?
Can you see the top
Mr. Secretary sir?
Can you see it?
And keeping them all here
piled up
I still don't understand
how we can all fit
on this spit of land
this postage stamp
Jean-Baptiste for example
rises to his feet, sure of himself
I'm going home to mama
he jumps in
disappears
what number is Jean-Baptiste
which number do I put
Mister Secretary sir
I don't know
me, general and president
charged with the census
I don't know
what number is Jean-Baptiste

(silenzio)

Non ci leggo

(silenzio)

Non ci leggo
signor Ministro

(silenzio)

Non ci leggo

(silenzio)

Eh no, proprio non ci leggo

(silenzio)

NON-CI-LEG-GOOO!

(silence)

I can't make it out

(silence)

I can't make it out
Mister Secretary sir

(silence)

I can't make it out

(silence)

I cannot make it out

(silence)

I-CAN'T-MAKE-IT-OOOUTTT!

---

[1] Silenzio! Silenzio! Basta!
[2] Silence! Silence! Enough!
[3] Basta, smettetela di fare tutto questo baccano. Smettetela di saltellare come i gin e i trickster. Fermatevi un po'. Basta!
[4] Enough, cut out all this uproar. Stop jumping around like djinns and tricksters. Stop it. Enough!

Voices in the Sea
On Marco Martinelli's *Rumore di acque*

FRANCO NASI

> Yes, as everyone knows, meditation and water are
> wedded forever.
>
> Herman Melville[1]

> And the soldiers wore around their neck or wrist
> a tag with their name and the number of their
> regiment to indicate who was who, and where to
> send a telegram of condolences, but if the explo-
> sion tore off their head or arm and the tag was
> lost, the military command would announce that
> they were unknown soldiers. . .
>
> Patrick Ouředník[2]

In its first founding manifestoes of the 1980s, Teatro delle Albe defined itself as "Politttttttical Theater," with seven t's, to de-clare with irreverent irony its distance from the era's reigning, ideologically muscle-bound political theater, turgid and smug in its certainties and judgments.[3] Because in Italian the word 'politi-co' means 'political' but the word 'polittico', with two t's, means 'polyptych' – that is, a painting consisting of multiple images – the invention of the ironic term 'politttttttico' also intended to trumpet the urgency of observing Italy's community (the *polis*) from multiple viewpoints, fixing a fiercely ingenuous gaze on a plural reality. Unafraid of finding surprise in the ordinary, the company declared that it would create theatrical actions com-

---

[1] Herman Melville, *Moby Dick* (Berkeley: U California P, 1979) 3.

[2] Patrick Ouředník, *Europeana. A Brief History of the Twentieth Century*, trans. Gerald Turner (Normal, IL: Dalkey Archive P, 2005) 3.

[3] Marco Martinelli, ed., *Ravenna africana* (Ravenna: Essegi, 1988) 7.

posed of multifaceted representations, aimed at an audience in search of questions rather than confirmation of received thought.

This heretical approach to politically committed theater carries on in *Rumore di acque*, the monologue composed in 2010 by Marco Martinelli, the playwright, director, and founder of the company established in 1983 together with Ermanna Montanari, Marcella Nonni, and Luigi Dadina.[4]

The story told in the play is not original. It is the tragically familiar account of the thousands of migrants who, setting out on broken-down and improvised boats from the shores of northern Africa, fail to make it to the coast of Europe and are swallowed by the Mediterranean Sea, now become a vast cemetery of the nameless dead.[5] It is a story that Italians in particular have come to know especially through television news reports, which first shock and then, through sheer repetition, gradually fold into the pattern of everyday life, another misfortune befalling people we don't know whose deaths don't affect us, like events in a movie. But theatre, by its nature a place where tragedy is re-presented and re-enacted, can make of these facts something much deeper and more powerful. Theatre draws its spectators into the eternal present of an action and makes them understand that what is taking place touches them intimately, transforming shock into personal trauma, a rupture of our idea of ourselves.[6]

But *Rumore di acque* does not consist solely of the wrenching representation of the lives and deaths of Yusuf, Sakinah, Jasmine, Obedience, Jean-Baptiste and the 77 nameless passengers, unknown soldiers, sliced to pieces by the rotors of the very ship sent to save them. There is also, in extreme closeup, the unhinged, psychotic, sadistic, cynical, fatalist, but also sympathetic and

---

[4] Marco Martinelli, *Rumore di acque* (Rome: Editoria & Spettacolo, 2010).
[5] The exact number of victims is unknown. Recent estimates presented to the Italian Senate speak of twenty thousand dead in the past twenty years.
[6] On the notion of trauma and the rupture of the subject, see Jacques Lacan, *The Four Fundamental Concepts of Psychoanalysis*, trans. Alan Sheridan (New York: W.W. Norton, 1981).

grieving spirit of the narrator, a schizoid General/Doorkeeper of an island of the dead, whose task is to gather and count the souls of the migrants who never make it to shore. Because at first he so resembles Qaddafi, with his uniform and dark glasses and ranks of medals on his chest, he appears far different from us. But at the same time, because he is so complex and contradictory, he necessarily resembles us and represents us. He draws us into the action along with him, making us complicit in the Mediterranean tragedy told through Martinelli's words and the voice of actor Alessandro Renda. The music of the Mancuso Brothers, rooted in the Sicilian folk tradition, serves as counterpoint to the narration, functionally similar to a Greek chorus singing of universal, unifying loss.

This epic tragedy, a rite in the form of a solo actor's narration, becomes a compact, compelling spectacle that unfolds in succeeding movements like a sonata: the *Stories* follow and balance one another in varying rhythm as they build toward a crescendo. Martinelli's text, furthermore, is threaded with internal references to the work and poetics of Teatro delle Albe. The topos of *Water* as a mirror of the self, and the *Voice* of the character-mask of an introverted crank, are repeated figures that merit exploration in order to more deeply comprehend this haunting play.

1. Stories

The General/Doorkeeper begins his monologue complaining: it's impossible to read the numbers that should identify each migrant soul. "Can anyone read this?" So he begins, mumbling and grumbling, his assigned task of identifying the dead. He seeks a number, a name, perhaps a scrap of story of a life gone forever. The monologue will end without resolution, but in place of a question, it will finally turn into a cry marked out in capital letters: "I-CAN'T-MAKE-IT-OOOUTTT!," as though he were refusing to carry on his duty to give names to the lost. In between these two moments, the piece consists largely of the reading of numbers, at times frenetic, at others minute, ordered, scientific. Through the numbers and with his declared principle that "science is interpretation," the General/Doorkeeper traces his way back into the life stories of some of the migrants. The first is the story of number 2917, Yusuf, from the Western Sahara. A young braggart, Yusuf learns to pilot his boss's boat on the calm waters of Naila Lagoon in Morocco, and quickly starts boasting of being able to cross the sea. But instead of leading the 16 people crammed onto his dinghy to freedom, he conveys them to their deaths: "Just outside the lagoon / A two meter wave / dinghy fills with water / Everyone drowns / Down to the bottom / Even the braggart / All over."

There are kabbalistic numbers that give witness to massacres of many at once, like the document numbered 7777 that identifies 77 migrants. Fallen into the water when their boat collapses, they hope to be saved by the arrival of an Italian military launch, but are sucked into the spinning rotors of the navy boat and sliced to pieces, due to the stupidity of the admiral's son who captains the Italian ship.

There's the story of number 44, Sakinah, one of the first to risk the voyage, together with 30 other Nigerian women, "little girls almost," likely destined for prostitution. But instead of finding themselves between silken sheets in white men's beds, they lay at the bottom of the sea, transformed by a harsh but lyrical Ovidian metamorphosis: "of their bones are coral made / those are pearls that were their eyes;" Martinelli borrows the words from Ariel in Shakespeare's *Tempest*, when the air sprite deceives Ferdinand into believing his father has died in the New World shipwreck.[7]

1111, another magical number, leads to the story of Jasmine, from Tunis, brave and stubborn, who survives a shipwreck only to become virtual slave to an old man, and is forced to serve even

---

[7] "Of his bones are coral made / those are pearls that were his eyes," Shakespeare, *The Tempest*, I, vv. 400-401.

his repulsive sexual demands. Jasmine, a tragic figure of *Life-in-Death*.

Then there's number 6132, Obedience, doomed obediently to pursue her fate. Escaping from bombs and certain torture in her homeland, she is destined instead to die at sea, her flesh a meal for sharks.

The last migrant, Jean-Baptiste, the youngest of all of the spirits evoked, resists for days on a raft adrift, but suddenly decides to return home to his mother: "All at once / Jean-Baptiste stands up / says, sure of himself / I'm going home to mama / and jumps in [. . .] / He swims a little / how far / twenty meters? / thirty? / then gets pulled down / disappears."

From these stories told with almost bureaucratic detachment, epitaphs in verse, brief sketches of lives and their abrupt conclusions, emerges gradually a restrained pity, intentionally veiled, that comes to climax in the caustic invective of the General/Doorkeeper directed against the fish, whom he accuses of being inhuman instruments of death: "Damn sharks / damn barracuda / damn mullet / and tuna / and leviathans / and behemoths / and killer whales / and giant turtles / damn John Dorys / damn blowfish / damn swordfish / and hammerheads / and tigerfish / and cutlassfish [. . .] / Sharks! / Pigs of the sea! / You devour everything / disfigure everything / and it's never enough for you! / Be a little more humane / sharks!" It's perhaps superfluous to point out the accelerating rhythm of the invective, clear even in this excerpt, which depends not only on the meter but on phonetic repetition, including alliteration, internal rhymes, anaphora, etc.[8] The wish expressed by the General/Doorkeeper at

---

[8] Martinelli continually and suddenly shifts linguistic registers, drawing now from the "high" poetic tradition, as in his use of the classical exhortation or apostrophe, and then without warning from pop culture slogans. His list of sea creatures includes the mythological leviathan, behemoth and giant turtle together with quite banal species such as the mullet and blowfish, in a manner reminiscent of his learned citation from Shakespeare's *Tempest* when the eyes

the end of his relentless sermon, that the sharks should be "more humane," is loaded with sarcasm about the fundamental nature of humankind. The fish are soulless instruments incapable of choice, with no more will than the rotor blades that slaughter the 77 migrants: "Can't blame them / the propellers I mean / Propellers have no brain." Humans instead should have brains and be capable of forethought; but apparently they are capable only of indifference and incompetence, allowing the sea floor to become an island of harvested souls. As though in a Greek tragedy, Fate seems to govern all, even evil itself. The evil of the world is taken as unassailable, a destiny hopeless to oppose. The General/Doorkeeper of the island of final welcome beneath the waves can do no more than grumble against the *daimons* of the underworld. After all, his duty is only to maintain the list of the dead. But as he tracks the numbers, so reminiscent of the ones tattooed on the arms of Nazi concentration camp prisoners, he cannot resist transforming them into narratives of individual lives. His muttering fabulations are the autistic soliloquy, both cynical and fearful, of an observer who above all is measuring himself. Accompanied by the choral voice of the Mancuso Brothers, the soliloquy blends with the "noise in the waters" that, like a great, indifferent mother, welcomes and rejects, unites and separates, bestowing both life and death.

2. Waters

Martinelli had already used the title, *Rumore di acque*, for one of his earliest plays, published in his first collection, in 1986, midway through the first decade of Teatro delle Albe (Fig. 1).[9] The published volume, which carries the same title, consists of three pieces produced by the company between 1983 and 1985, when they developed plays adapted from the novels of Philip K.

---

of the Nigerian girls turn into pearls. Crude realism mixes with canonical lyricism, following the polylingual model invented by Dante in his *Inferno*.
[9] Marco Martinelli, *Rumore di acque. Scritture teatrali* (Ravenna: Essegi, 1986).

Dick. In nightmaric works that run a razor's edge between science fiction and hyperrealism, Dick described contemporary society with its apocalyptic urban landscapes, the overlapping of fact and fiction, confusion between the real and its technological replicants, between human and android. Rather than exploring deep space, Dick penetrates the depthless interiors of his characters, who often find themselves at sea in the face of catastrophe. For the Albe company in that era, their native coastal city of Ravenna seemed set on a path of self-destruction, with its Byzantine basilicas, ancient mausoleums and historic pines forced to share the land with mefitic, infernal petroleum refineries. Dick's work thus offered an inspiring vocabulary of apocalypse to draw from as they embodied their own vision.

The first Albe play named *Rumore di acque* stages the story of a platoon of soldiers in search of a replicant deserter. Unable to find the replicant, they turn instead to an innocent local inhabitant named Galy Gay and try to convince him to take the android's place so as to allow them to get off the hook with their superior officers. The play is set in Ravenna after the Third World War, a nuclear Armageddon that took place in the mid-twenty-first century. While Ravenna remains the official name of the city, the war's survivors instead call it Rha-ama:

> In the public record the city's name is Ravenna. But after the Third, everything is changed; the old names for things echo in a void, so everyone calls it Rha-ama. A Phoenician word meaning "noise in the waters," the name arose in ancient times when it was a village built on stilts over a salty estuary at the sea's edge; a gray Venice made of wooden slats. The war's survivors restored the name Rha-ama because the waters had returned, after millennia: vertical waters, this time, radioactive rains.[10]

---

[10] Martinelli, *ibidem.*

In the very etymology of the name of the city of Ravenna, therefore, we find that "noise in the waters" that gives its title to two texts written twenty-five years apart. Like the sea, water functions as an archetype, but rather than a means of purification, it is the sign of the outrage that humankind has committed against the planet. In the first *Rumore*, the water falls, but it is radioactive, destroying the earth rather than making it fertile, forcing its inhabitants to close in on themselves, barricaded in their houses. It is an infernal rain, like that described by Dante in Canto VI of the *Inferno*:

> Io sono al terzo cerchio, della piova
> Etterna, maledetta, fredda e greve;
> regola e qualità mai non l'è nova.
> Grandine grossa, acqua tinta e neve
> Per l'aere tenebroso si riversa;
> pute la terra che questo riceve. (*Inferno*, VI, 7-12)

> I am in the third circle, place of eternal
> accursed, cold and thudding rain
> which in density and force is never new.
> Large hailstones, dirty rainwater, and snow
> course down through the murky air,
> the ground that receives them stinks.[11]

This is the circle presided over by Cerberus. Farther along in his *Rumore* of 1986, Martinelli puts several tercets of Dante into the mouth of one of his soldiers, referencing the three-headed monster with vermillion eyes ("O caciati del ciel, gente dispetta . . ." *Inferno*, IX, 91-99). The use of Dante's *Inferno* is not casual, but flanks the adaptation of Philip K. Dick's novel. The soldier who insults his comrades is disgusted by their indolence: they are in the middle of the Adriatic aboard a maritime junk, headed for

---

[11] Translation by Galway Kinnell in *Dante's Inferno. Translations by Twenty Contemporary Poets*, Daniel Halpern, ed. (Hopewell, NJ: Ecco Press, 1993) 26.

Dalmatia. But instead of rowing, all they do is chatter aimlessly while the surrounding sea is mute:

> The junk is immobile on the putrid, red broth, the night without wind: they are immobile, as though in a painted ship on a painted sea.[12]

The sea is rotten too, like the radioactive rain. This literary image is taken verbatim from an Italian translation of another epic poem, *The Ancient Mariner*, by Coleridge. With dazzling, hypnotic eyes, the protagonist compels the young wedding guests to listen to the tale of his guilt and never ending expiation:

> Day after day, day after day,
> We stuck, nor breath nor motion;
> As idle as a painted ship
> Upon a painted ocean. (II, 115-118)

The sea in the first *Rumore di acque* is also immobile, as though in a painting, an artistic fiction. An image of a painted image describes reality.

There are homologies in the descriptions of the sea in both versions of *Rumore di acque* that lead back to Coleridge's poem. The sea is a place of contradiction; a place to cross over on the way to a new life, but also the site of immobility and death, a realm both water and wasteland:

> Water, water, every where,
> And all the boards did shrink;
> Water, water, every where,
> Nor any drop to drink. (II, 119-122)

---

[12] Marco Martinelli, *Rumore di acque. Scritture teatrali* (Ravenna: Essegi, 1986) 141.

So goes the famous quatrain that immediately follows the citation given above. In his 2010 *Rumore*, Martinelli reuses Coleridges image of the contradictory sea:

> Per giorni, settimane
> Nel buio della notte
> Ghiaccio e tenebre
> Nel sole del meriggio
> Arsura

> For days, weeks
> In the dark of night
> Ice and blackness
> Blazing sun
> Scorching thirst

Still more literally comes the description of little Jean-Baptiste adrift in a rubber raft, deciding to return home to his mother by throwing himself hopelely into the arms of the sea:

> solo acqua tutto attorno
> l'orizzonte
> il cielo
> sembrano anche loro d'acqua
> niente più da mangiare
> niente più da bere
> sei in mezzo a tutta quell'acqua
> e non puoi berne una goccia.

> nothing but water everywhere
> the horizon
> the sky
> seem water too
> nothing left to eat
> nothing left to drink
> you're in the middle of all that water
> and you can't drink a drop

The Mediterranean turns up often throughout Martinelli's work, as a body martyred by the belligerent stupidity of human-kind. In *Bonifica. Polittico in sette quadri (Reclamation. Polyptych in Seven Paintings)*, staged first in 1989, appears a character named Arterio – an invention of Teatro delle Albe, a sort of archetypal mask figure like those in commedia dell'arte, earthy and rooted, cynical and paradoxical, awkwardly pragmatic and rationalist, lover of order and endless complainer – who listens to the sea as it wheezes asthmatically (Fig. 2). The sea "breathes heavily like a dying beast," and Arterio wants to put it out of its misery by burying it under a coating of cement. Here too the sea appears as a *locus horridus*, another ring of Dante's hell, inhabited by carnivorous fish, dragons and monsters, or becomes a desert of radioactive rain. The sea is a stagnant swamp, an underwater boneyard. It does not act; it merely *is*. It bears the actions of mankind, and thus becomes mankind's mirror. The sea is not the cause of the death of the immigrants. Others must answer for what the sea merely gathers: humans must answer, whose inhuman actions are motivated by economic interest, global indifference, and purposeful silence:

> Nessuno lo verrà a sapere [. . .]
> Agli uomini sarà chiesto il silenzio [. . .]
> una bella colata di silenzio

> No one will know [. . .]
> Silence from the crew [. . .]
> A cement coating of silence

Thus the sea becomes a place onto which the self is projected, a mirror before which our monstrous General/Doorkeeper reveals himself to himself. In *Moby Dick*, Melville writes:

> Why upon your first voyage as a passenger, did you yourself feel such a mystical vibration, when first told that you and

your ship were now out of sight of land? Why did the old Persians hold the sea holy? Why did the Greeks give it a separate deity, and own brother of Jove? Surely all this is not without meaning. And still deeper the meaning of that story of Narcissus, who because he could not grasp the tormenting, mild image he saw in the fountain, plunged into it and was drowned. But that same image, we ourselves see in all rivers and oceans. It is the image of the ungraspable phantom of life; and this is the key to it all.[13]

In John Huston's famous adaptation of the tale, these words of Melville are synthesized into an aphorism: "The sea, where each man as in a mirror finds himself."[14]

3. *Voice*

Like the sea, the protagonist of the 2010 *Rumore di acque* grows from important counterparts in other works by Teatro delle Albe. I am thinking here of the genealogy of characters who lead up to the creation of the General/Doorkeeper who tallies the dead in his underworld cemetery. This guardian figure has numerous corollaries in literary history, from Charon to the porter of Macbeth's castle, but he has many "prefigurations" also in Teatro delle Albe, beginning with his closest chronological twin, the "doorman who dreams of being the devil" or "the devil who dreams of being the doorman" in *Leben*, of 2006 (Fig. 3).[15]

---

[13] Herman Melville, *Moby Dick* (Berkeley, U California P, 1979), 4.

[14] The screenplay of the 1956 film of *Moby Dick* was composed by John Huston together with Ray Bradbury.

[15] This work derives from a rereading of *Scherz, Satire, Ironie und tiefere Bedeutung* (1822), a grotesque composition for theatre by the German playwright Christian D. Grabbe, that tells the story of a miniature devil who has fallen to earth among Enlightenment scientists. In the Albe version, which debuted in 2006 with the title *Scherzo, Satira, Ironia e Significato profondo* ("Comedy, Satire, Irony and Deep Meaning"), Grabbe's plot is threaded into another that involves a board meeting of investors in a super-efficient, inhuman firm that works in porno-tourism ("suitcase girls"). In this second plot thread, actor Alessandro Renda, who plays the devil, is also the doorman at Leben, Inc.,

The earliest version, and most similar in character to the General/Doorkeeper of *Rumore* 2010, is probably the character-mask of Arterio: individualist, pig-headedly rational, simple-mindedly pragmatic, whining, sanguine, and corpulent both in body and speech that pours directly from his belly in a dry, cutting dialect. Ambiguous and as sentimental as a peasant, Arterio is bound to the mother he venerates but wants to overpower. He is intensely diffident toward the new, the different, the other, toward anything that does not pertain to his own worn-out civilization. After a first appearance in *Bonifica*, the Arterio character returns in another Albe play, *I Refrattari*, of 1992 (Fig. 4). The action here begins with the arrival at the home of Arterio and Daura, his wife, of a strange living creature seemingly inspired by the replicants of Philip K. Dick, a Lucciola Pianta Topo ("Firefly Plant Rat") escaped from a laboratory. Arterio reacts to this apparition with a sharp reproach toward his mother in Romagnol dialect: "A t'e' degh tot i dé, sëra la pôrta!" ("I tell you every day: shut the door!"). For Arterio, the only solution to the invasive presence of the other, whether it comes from a lab, from the south, or from Africa, is to keep the door shut, or to dream of escaping to somewhere impossible, such as the moon.

Another character hostile to the other and shut up in himself is Pantalone, the traditional mask of the commedia dell'arte, a central figure in a scenario by Carlo Goldoni adapted and staged by Teatro delle Albe in 1993 with the title, *I ventidue infortuni di Mor Arlecchino* ("The Twenty-Two Misfortunes of Moor Arlecchino") (Fig. 5). In commedia generally and in the Albe's adaptation, the antagonists of the avaricious, lecherous old man are always represented by the new, the different, the young.

The characters Martinelli invents are strongly determined by the actors in his company who will play the roles, and their spe-

---

run by the harsh, arrogant Condolcezza (Ermanna Montanari. [In Italian the allusory name means "with sweetness"]), who will turn out to be the devil's mother. This "suitcase operetta," so named in its subtitle, was published in 2009 by Editoria & Spettacolo with its new title, *Leben*.

cific qualities grow from the close collaboration between writer and actor during the development process.[16] It is thus no surprise that there should be certain profoud affinities between Pantalone and Arterio, as both roles were developed for and by Luigi Dadina. By a further extension of this same affinity, two deeply interesting theatrical texts staged by the Albe under Martinelli's direction, *Zitti tutti* (*Everyone Shut up*, 1993) by Raffello Baldini, and *Stranieri* (*Foreigners*, 2008) by Antonio Tarantino, feature lead characters similar to Arterio (Fig. 6).

Fascinating from a literary viewpoint, *Zitti tutti* is the monologue in Romagnol dialect of a solitary wealthy man with an excess of free time and its concurrent sense of emptiness. He isolates himself from the world and speaks of it as something extraneous and impossible to make sense of. Even his family is foreign to him: "at dinner, sometimes, eating like that, everyone by himself, I feel like a foreigner."[17] The text consists of the character's neverending, syntactically uninterrupted complaining, with endlessly overlapping thoughts, ranting, and repetitive banalities that contradict one another. The nameless character's soliloquy admits no dialogue with others. Toward the end of the piece, he says that people criticize him for speaking to himself like a madman. But he answers the charge by saying that no one would understand him anyway, because the others don't know anything, leaving him no alternative than to talk to himself. But even this self-address becomes unbearable to him, leaving him naked among his inconclusive contradictions and incapacity to take action. He arrives finally at the tragic last scene in which he shoots his own image in the mirror:

---

[16] See, Gerardo Guccini, "Martinelli autore e il multidramma delle Albe" in F. Montanino, ed. *Marco Martinelli* (Rome: Editoria & Spettacolo, 2006).

[17] "che ma la tèvla, dal vólti, a magne, acsè, ognun par còunt sóvv, u m pèr d'ès un furistìr"; Raffello Baldini, *Zitti tutti!* Italian translation by Raffello Baldini (Milan: Ubulibri, 1993) 74-5.

Franco Nasi

Everyone shut up, shut up now, eh, you're afraid, chickens,
you don't get it, none of you, you never got it, I'm the one who
should shut up, (*he goes to the mirror, watches himself*), but instead I talk talk talk (*he takes a step back*), and go on talking,
go on (*another step back*), I should shut up, (*another step
back*), shut up, enough (*still another step back, staring at himself*), shut up, shut up, shut up (*points the double-barreled shot-
gun at the mirror*), Silence! (*he shoots, the mirror shatters.
Blackout.*)[18]

In *Stranieri*, the intense text by Antonio Tarantino, the lead
character is also nameless.[19] As it opens, a solitary, aged old father hostile to the world "wanders around an empty room," curs-
ing at someone beyond the door: "What are you knocking for / I
won't open for anyone / The door is barred." He is angry at immigrants ("All criminals [. . .], they don't want to work [. . .] / I've
got my hunting rifle [. . .] / I won't open / No open / Go away"),
impatient with his foreign-born daughter-in-law and nephew
("Who can understand / They whisper together / I don't exist for
them / They're different"), and opposed to his son's study of phi-
losophy, which he considers mere empty words. Alternating with
short verses (similar to the 2010 *Rumore di acque*) come dia-
logues in prose taking place just outside the door of the room
between his dead wife and son, who knock and want to come in.
They have come to take away the father, who refuses to recognize
them even when they finally enter and speak to him directly.
They find him, delirious in front of the mirror, as he questions
his own identity and worries that "the law of gravity is losing its

---

[18] Zitti tutti, adès a sté zétt, ehn, 'i paéura, patàca, ch'a n capì gnént, niséun, a n'i
mai capì gnént, a so mè ch'ò da stè zétt, (*va vicino allo specchio, si guarda*), che
invìci a zcòrr, a zcòrr, (*arretra un passo*), e piò ch'a zcòrr, (*d'un altro passo*) ò da
stè zétt, zétt, (*d'un altro passo*) sta zétt, basta, (*arretra d'un altro passo, sempre
fissandosi*) sta zétt, zétt, sta zétt, (*punta la doppietta contro lo specchio*) silenzio!
(*spara, lo specchio va in frantumi. Buio*). Ivi, pp.76-79.
[19] Antonio Tarantino, "Stranieri" in *La casa di Ramallah e altre conversazioni*
(Milan: Ubulibri, 1996).

123

power over me." His wife and son have become strangers to him. His wife says:

> Why do you find it so strange that we strangers are strange to one another? We all presume to know everyone inside out, but it is exactly this strange concept that makes us so foreign one to another [. . .] And the more enchained we are by tight bonds, the stronger our conviction – that we have nothing more to learn from the other – aggravates our prejudice, impeding true awareness and rendering us truly all strangers to all.

Since these male figures constitute a sort of prefiguration of the General/Doorkeeper of *Rumore*, we should turn our attention to the actor, Alessandro Renda, whose voice and body bring the character to life. We have already made reference to the way Martinelli's compositional method flows directly from the interaction between the writer/director and his actors. Although every actor must follow his or her own *daimon*, his or her own original, unique "vocation," it is tempting to think of Renda's General as a child of the two original "masks" of Teatro delle Albe, Arterio/Dadina and Daura/Montanari. Renda in fact has played this couple's son in the staging of Tarantino's *Stranieri*, but the younger actor's debt to these first-generation Albe actors is still deeper. We have already spoken of Luigi Dadina's creation of the characters of Arterio and Pantalone, and should now devote some attention to the numerous pieces that Ermanna Montanari has invented, serving as the dominant vocal element, from *Confine* ("Border," from a text by Marco Belpoliti, 1986. Fig. 7) to *Rosvita* (inspired by the work of the medieval canoness Hrotsvitha/Roswitha of Gandersheim, 1991. Fig. 8), *Cenci* (taken from both Shelley and Artaud, 1993), *Luş* (text by Nevio Spadoni, 1995. Fig. 9), *L'isola di Alcina* ("Alcina's Island," again by Spadoni, dervied from Ariosto, 2000), *La mano* ("The Hand," text by Luca Doninelli, 2005), to a new version of *Rosvita* (2008. Fig. 10). Recalling the performances of these works in memory or listening to the tapes, it's impossible not to be amazed by Ermanna Montanari's work on the human voice, remarkable not only for the wide gamut of notes and intensities it discovers, but for the incredible variety of resonances she uses, from throat voice to stomach voice, head voice to belly voice. The voice is rebellious and deep; in one moment it scratches and in the next it sings, but without ever imitating *bel canto*. Above all, her voice that never limits itself to serving as the mere vehicle of language, asserting instead its own autonomous values. Paul Zumthor's distinction between orality and vocality is certainly relevant here: "I define 'orality' as the voice that functions as a bearer of language; 'vocality' is the sum of the activities and values inherent to the voice itself, independent of language."[20] In much of her work, Ermanna Montanari's research focuses especially on vocality, communicating intense emotions through a language that has no lexical or syntactic clarity for listeners, because the language it speaks is either unknown or rationally incomprehensible. Two pieces performed in Romagnol dialect, *Luş* and *Isola di Alcina*, have been received with praise by foreign audiences who do not speak Italian, much less a regional dialect of Italian, because the vocal expressiveness is so direct and of such immediacy as to reveal the limitations of standard semantics.

The score performed by Renda in *Rumore di acque* does not forgo semantics in favor of a total autonomy of vocality, but Ermanna Montanari's example is evident both when the General/Doorkeeper's voice becomes most demoniacal and when, in a starkly lower, whsipered tone, we sense the speaker's repressed grief. The contrasting resonances used by Renda reinforce the compact complexity of Martinelli's words.

The text, in effect, becomes a musical score, especially when the narrative voice counterpoints the voices and instruments of the Mancuso Brothers (Fig. 11). The duo sings the lament of a

---

[20] Paul Zumthor, "Preface" in Corrado Bologna, *Flatus vocis. Metafisica e antropologia della voce* (Bologna: il Mulino, 2000, 2nd ed.) VII, IX.

city, aiming to "harpoon" with their voices those who have "drowned in the Straight of Sicily." The brothers describe their intentions with these words:

> To us it seemed that we somehow spoke the same language as all those people buried in the depths. We tried to reach that language by pushing our vocal modulation to its limits, with chordal doubling, forcing the spectrum of vocal emission to its widest possible limits [. . .] We felt we were speaking the same language, when words become a vocal gesture that communicates by subcutaneous vibrations, shaking the internal organs. Our Sicilian has always been a wild, strange language.[21]

Epilogue. The Drowned and the Indifferent

The character Arterio, the old man of *Zitti tutti*, the old father of *Stranieri*, the General/Doorkeeper: they all complain and grumble, shut up inside themselves, refractory toward a world populated by foreigners and an ever-more-foreign family. At the same time, they are plagued by a stubborn incapacity to listen that they scream aloud. During their soliloquies before the mirror, they are visited by the apparitions of others, by those they insist on excluding. A leaden sense of guilt drives them to denounce their own inadequacy. The thought they won't admit to torments them; they refuse to acknowledge it but it bears down on them with every step.

In closing these reflections, Primo Levi's poem "Il superstite" ("The Survivor") comes to mind, from his 1984 collection *Ad ora incerta* ("At an Uncertain Hour"). The poem is constructed around two texts Martinelli has also used, as we have seen: "The Ancient Mariner" by Coleridge and Dante's *Inferno*. Suddenly and irresistably, "at an uncertain hour," the old sailor is compelled to tell everyone he meets the story of his unmotivated

---

[21] Enzo and Lorenzo Mancuso, "Parlare la stessa lingua" ("Speaking the Same Language") in Marco Martinelli, *Rumore di acque* (Rome: Editoria & Spettacolo), 69-70.

murder of the albatross and the curse that has followed upon it. Levi feels like the Ancient Mariner: he too is suddenly, unexpectedly overcome with the need to tell the cursed story of the extermination camp. Different from Coleridge's mariner, Levi does not feel responsible for causing the disgrace, which has befallen him; rather, he feels guilty for having survived. In a nightmare vision he sees those who perished there. Levi closes his poem with a verse from Dante, taken from the circle of the damned who betrayed their hosts (Canto XXXIII). These souls are sent to hell even before they die, their souls condemned to eternally expiate their sin in the ice of Cocytus. On Earth, meanwhile, a devil has taken the place of their soul and moves the body as though alive, making it eat and drink and sleep and put on clothes:

> *Dopo di allora, ad ora incerta,*
> Since then, at an uncertain hour,
> That agony returns:
> And until he finds who'll listen
> His heart within him burns.
>
> Once more he sees his companions' faces
> Livid in the first faint light,
> Gray with cement dust,
> Nebulous in the mist,
> Tinged with death in their uneasy sleep.
> At night, under the heavy burden
> Of their dreams, their jaws move,
> Chewing a nonexistent turnip.
> 'Stand back, leave me alone, submerged people,
> Go away. I haven't dispossessed anyone,
> Haven't usurped anyone's bread.
> No one died in my place. No one.
> Go back into your mist.
> It's not my fault if I live and breathe,
> Eat, drink, sleep and put on clothes.'[22]

---

[22] Original Italian edition, Primo Levi, *Ad ora incerta* (Garzanti Editore: Milan,

The General/Doorkeeper of the underwater island where the souls gather, this Charon who counts nametags, is indeed responsible, and seems to gradually acquire awareness of his guilt as he recounts the tales of the dead (Fig. 12). Just as he is, we spectators are responsible too. *Rumore di acque* is the epic tragedy of the brutal death of thousands of migrants, but also of our wretched, inhuman impotence, incarnated in the General/ Doorkeeper who mirrors himself in those fatal waters. "At an uncertain hour," *voices of the waters* and *voices in the waters* surface inevitably and mournfully demand to have their story told.

Translated by Thomas Simpson

1984). English translation, Primo Levi, *Collected Poems*, trans. by Ruth Feldman and Brian Swann (London: Faber & Faber, 1988) 64. The first verse of Levi's poem consists of a citation from Coleridge's poem, but Levi alters the British poet's first-person address ("And till my ghastly take is told / This heart within me burns") to third-person (E se non trova chi lo ascolti / Gli brucia in petto il cuore"). We have rendered these lines as, "And until he finds who'll listen / His heart within him burns."

PHOTOS

Figure 1 • P. 130

Rumore di acque, 1985. Pictured: Marco Martinelli, Ermanna Montanari, Luigi Dadina (photo Andrea Fabbri Cossarini)

Figure 2 • P. 131

Bonifica, 1989. Pictured: Ermanna Montanari (photo Paolo Volponi)

Figure 3 • P. 132

Leben, 2006. Pictured: Ermanna Montanari, Alessandro Renda (photo Christian Contin)

Figure 4 • P. 133

I Refrattari, 1992. Pictured: Ermanna Montanari, Luigi Dadina (photo Massimo Fiorentini)

Figure 5 • P. 134

I 22 infortuni di Mor Arlecchino, 1993. Pictured: Mor Awa Niang in the role of Arlecchino (photo Marco Caselli Nirmal)

Figure 6 • P. 135

Stranieri, 2008. Pictured: Luigi Dadina (photo Claire Pasquier)

Figure 7 • P. 136

Confine, 1986. Pictured: Marco Martinelli, Ermanna Montanari (photo Enrico Sotgiu)

Figure 8 • P. 137

Rosvita, 1991. Pictured: Ermanna Montanari (photo Marco Caselli Nirmal)

Figure 9 • P. 138

Lus, 1995. Pictured: Ermanna Montanari (photo Corelli and Fiorentini)

Figure 10 • P. 139

Rosvita, 2008. Pictured: Ermanna Montanari (photo Fabio Cito)

Figure 11 • P. 140

Rumore di acque, 2010. Pictured: The Mancuso Brothers, Alessandro Renda (photo Luca Bolognese)

Figure 12 • P. 141

Rumore di acque, 2010. Pictured: Alessandro Renda (photo Claire Pasquier)

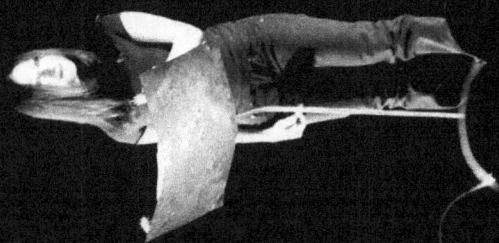

CONVERSIONE DI TAIDE

Postcards from a Mediterranean Solid Sea
The Depths of "Migration Management" at the Blue Frontier

Almost 20,000 people have been reported dead[1] while trying to reach the European Union crossing the Mediterranean Sea, since 1998. In these few pages I trace some of the interrupted journeys, the growing economic interests, and the border politics of this marine cemetery through a series of situated vignettes.

1. *Via dei Cimiteri marini and Piazza Basta morti nel Mediterraneo: The Urban Core of Deaths in Open Sea*
    During a day of action, the feminist collective Leventicinqueundici scattered downtown Milan with contesting street signs, such as 'Marine Cemeteries Avenue' and 'Stop Deaths in the Mediterranean Square,'[2] literally taking the tragedy of migrants in the Mediterranean to the streets. The political statement was clear: migrants' deaths at sea are no accident. Taking a chance with smugglers on overcrowded small boats is often the only choice for those fleeing famine, persecution, dire poverty, war, and political unrest.[3] Moreover, the protest suggested, in one of the world's busiest and best-monitored seas in the world, ship-

---

[1] This is an underestimate, not taking into account the unreported destiny of those who went missing trying to reach the European shore. (Source: Fortress Europe, http://fortresseurope.blogspot.com).

[2] Leventicinqueundici, *Rinominiamo le nostre città*, http://leventicinqueundici. noblogs.org/?p=1242.

[3] Access to Europe, even for a short stay, is contingent on the accident of birth: a passport from an African or a Middle Eastern country, for instance, requires a visa to certify that the traveler is legally employed at home, in good financial standing, and in good health (additional requirements apply on a country basis). To seek asylum or other forms of international protection in a European country a foreigner needs to file a request in person at the competent office of that European country (discussions are undergoing at the EU level to possibly change this provision).

wrecks can't be glossed over as a natural calamity, triggering facile humanitarian tears and vaporizing political responsibilities.
Instead, the tragedy of deaths in the Mediterranean points to
a *solid* sea: a sea whose depths are filled by people's remnants and
whose bottoms are scattered with shipwrecks;[4] and also a sea so
embedded in the politics of the continents that it bears their solidity and interests, binding the Mediterranean shores together as
a policy region. But the solidity of the Mediterranean region may
go unnoticed until it begins to break apart, as it did in March
2011. As European leaders were getting ready to join the NATO
intervention in the Libyan civil war, Muammar Qaddafi spelled
out some of the deals of this "migration management"[5] region:

I want to make myself understood: if one threatens Libya, [...]
[y]ou will have immigration, thousands of people will invade
Europe from Libya. And there will no longer be anyone to stop
them.[6]

As a matter of fact, many Sub-Saharan citizens previously
living in Libya and now housed in refugee processing centers in
Italy, tell of being forcefully removed by Qaddafi's militia, kid-
napped, stripped of their documents and forced to set sail to Italy.
And many others tell the story of deciding to flee a country at
war, similarly leaving on fishing boats towards Italy.

But how was Qaddafi in the position to threaten Europe with
a migratory invasion? The threat was rooted in Mediterranean
politics: throughout the 90s and 00s, dictators like Qaddafi in
Libya, Ben Ali in Tunisia, and Mubarak in Egypt, took on the
chore to combat migration to Europe in exchange for economic
investment in their countries, enforcing preemptive border operations for the EU and/or accepting mass deportations of undoc-
umented African migrants. This is the "migration management"

---

[4] Multiplicity, *Solid Sea*, http://www.multiplicity.it/home.swf.
[5] The notion of 'migration management' was elaborated by Bimal Ghosh in his
work for the United Nations Commission on Global Governance in the 90s.
[6] Frenzen, N. (2011, March 7). Gaddafi: If Libya is threatened, thousands of
immigrants will invade Europe from Libya, http://migrantsatsea.wordpress.
com/.

region that has been organized across the Mediterranean, casting away migrants and refugees on the southern shore: a "Euro-med neighbourhood"[7] of atrocious spatial fixes for "abject cosmopolitans"[8] and a solid sea of policy traffic and political deals struck on expendable lives.

Whereas anti-immigration sentiment in Europe crystallizes on the trope of nation-state border-crossing and results in calls for stopping immigrants at entry-points, the EU is at the vanguard of experiments of "externalization" of its frontier: the delocalization of border-work away from the European borderline – i.e. away from the country of destination and to countries of departure or transit. That is, the EU purchases the services of bad cops from the other shore to contain out-migrations. But as European borders 'migrated' to the African continent, protocols for border operations and migrant rights did not travel with them. As a result, this *war on migrants*, conveniently conducted away from Europe, resulted in an escalation of violations, abuses and violence.

So, for instance, by 2009-2010 the Lampedusa[9] route into Europe had closed off as a result of EU and Italian agreements with Northern African countries. Whereas in 2008 over 30,000 migrants had arrived at Lampedusa island, numbers fell sharply in 2009 and 2010[10] after the signing of the Friendship Treaty between Italy and Libya in 2008, a colonial reparation of $5 billion for the damages inflicted by Italy on Libya. In exchange for the reparation, Libya granted Italy privileged access to the oil and large-scale infrastructure sectors, and also promised to prevent

---

[7] With the expression 'Euro-Med neighbourhood' the EU indicates its 'external policy' area in the Mediterranean, including Northern African and Middle Eastern countries. See: http://www.enpi-info.eu/.

[8] Breckenridge, C. et al (Eds) (2002). *Cosmopolitanism* (Durham, NC: Duke University Press). Nyers, P. (2003). "Abject Cosmopolitanism: The Politics of Protection in the Anti-deportation Movement," *Third World Quarterly* 24(6): 1069-1093.

[9] Lampedusa Island is the southernmost tip of Italy, south of Sicily, and served as a maritime entry into Europe for migrants from other Mediterranean shores.

[10] Numbers fell to 2,947 in 2009 and 459 in 2010. (Source: http://assembly. coe.int/CommitteeDocs/2011/amahlarg03_REV2_2011. pdf).

so called "illegal" immigration to Italy. "We will get more oil and fewer illegal migrants," Prime Minister Berlusconi triumphantly declared at the signing of the treaty. The flagship of this border-work was the pushback policy: upon interception at sea, migrants of any nationality were returned to Libya and locked up in Libyan detention centers whose inhumane conditions were well known. It was also a known fact that Libya is not a signatory of the 1951 Refugee Convention and has no asylum system in place. Eritreans intercepted by Libyan forces while trying to reach Europe to seek asylum describe conditions in these Libyan centers: "78 people were housed in a 19x26 feet cell, [...] sleeping on the floor, our head by someone else's feet. They starved us, at times eight of us had to share one plate of rice [...] Policemen would get in the cell, take a woman and abuse her in front of everybody."[11] The European Court of Human Rights condemned Italy for the pushback policy in 2012.

Proxies and practices to enforce the EU border abroad change according to the country and the terms of bilateral agreements. In Tunisia, for instance, the focus is on the regulatory side, with draconian penalties for those helping people migrate and very strict visa requirements for leaving the country, with a provision breaching the fundamental right of any person "to leave any country, including his own."[12] The short 70-mile stretch of sea between Italy and Tunisia has been turned into an insurmountable barrier, locking Tunisians up in a Euro-Med captivity, both under Ben Ali and afterwards.[13]

Smugglers profit on these policies and lives are lost at sea. There is nothing natural about this marine tragedy and Mediterranean graveyard, as the sign 'Stop Deaths in the Mediterranean Square' suggested, land-marking with such a protest the European city of Milan. Any call for saving lives in the Mediterranean

---

[11] Del Grande, G. (2009). Guantanamo Libia, in M. Carsetti & A. Triulzi (Eds), *Come un uomo sulla terra* (Milano: Infinito Edizioni).

[12] Assembly, UN General (1948). *Universal Declaration of Human Rights. Resolution Adopted by the General Assembly,* Article 13.

[13] After the fall of Ben Ali, Italy and Tunisia signed new agreements covering immigration issues in 2011 and 2012.

that does not deal with the politics of the European border is, at best, shortsighted, albeit in humanitarian disguise.

2. "Be a little more humane, sharks!": The Humanitarian Militarization of the Mediterranean

In the first two weeks of October 2013, the call to save lives came after two tragic shipwrecks, just a few days from one another. On October 3, *three hundred and sixty six* people, mainly from Somalia and Eritrea, died less than a quarter mile from Lampedusa Island when their boat capsized, in the biggest single loss of life ever reported in the Mediterranean of migrant mobility. A few days later, on October 11, *two hundred and sixty* Syrians, including about *one hundred* children, died as their boat sank 70 miles south of Lampedusa. The massacre brought the daily necro-politics of Mediterranean mobility to global media attention.

What became of these people afterwards, as they finally landed in Europe, whether in body bags or on their feet? The dead were bestowed posthumous citizenship and state funerals were announced for them (but never in fact carried out). Survivors, on the other hand, were locked up, charged with illegal entry and denied the possibility to attend their relatives' and friends' funerals. The division of the shipwrecks' passengers between honorary dead citizens *and* deportable survivors exemplifies the conflation of humanitarian labels with policing agendas that is becoming a hallmark of European immigration policies. Harsh enforcement and military intervention are wrapped in an ethical package and given a convenient human rights label.

One such intervention came as the political response to the October shipwrecks: on October 14, 2013, amid a still shaken public opinion, the Italian government launched a "military and humanitarian mission" in the Sicily Channel, problematically termed Mare Nostrum,[14] with the double goal, as the Ministry of

---

[14] Italian politicians defended the name as metaphorically alluding to an assumption of responsibility for the tragedies in the Mediterranean. However, the history of such name – in its Roman Empire and Fascist deployments – points

Glenda Garelli

the Interior put it, to protect migrants' lives and to grant "control over migration flows,"[15] to prevent deaths at sea and to block so called "illegal" entry into Europe. The Mare Nostrum mission came in full marketing hype, with obsessive, enthusiastic coverage of the military convoy. The deployment is indeed huge: an 8,000 ton amphibious assault ship, five more naval vessels, helicopters and an airplane equipped with infrared night vision, plus unmanned drones. Media attention converged on the features of the military deployment, framing the response to the tragedy in the Mediterranean as a depoliticized matter of force, the technical muscle necessary to combat so called "illegal"[16] immigration and to out-scale natural catastrophes at sea.

And the marketing worked: a big part of Italian public opinion signed on, letting go even of the 'we can't afford it' refrain that is recently also underpinning center-left anti-immigration sentiment. An astonishing concession if one looks at the figures: Mare Nostrum was announced to come, for the Italian taxpayer, at a monthly cost of 4 million Euros, according to the Ministry of the Interior; the estimate was re-assessed at 10.5 million Euros a month by the Confederation of Italian Industries newspaper and at 12 million Euros by the technical magazine *Analisi Difesa*. In March 2014, a few months into the mission, a point of order finally established a monthly cost between 12 and 14 million Euros a month.[17] A lot of money, which adds to funds already allocated for border enforcement in this area of the Mediterranean[18].

---

to the appropriative legacy of the Italian claim to the Mediterranean, as the grammar of 'Mare Nostrum' also indisputably clarifies.

[15] Interview, Source: *Il Sole 24 ore*, 14 ottobre 2013.

[16] In critical migration studies, the notion of "illegal immigration" has been contested. In this case, the attribution is particularly problematic as the passengers were potential asylum seekers.

[17] Molteni, N. (2014). *Atto Camera. Interrogazione a risposta scritta 4-04164*, Seduta no. 196, 24 marzo 2014. Source: http://banchedati.camera.it/sinda catoispettivo_17/showXhtml.asp?highLight=0&idAtto=16250&stile=7.

[18] Some of the other resources allocated in 2013: Italy, 10.5 million Euros ('Missione Italiana in Libia' (MIL) and Guardia di Finanza operations); EU, 114 million for Frontex operations (Frontex is the EU external borders agency). Source:

Mare Nostrum has certainly been engaging in rescue operations in open sea since its launching. However, the humanitarian component of the operation may stop at the blue frontier for some migrants, if, as Interior Minister Alfano suggested, those rescued "will not necessarily be brought to Italy." As I write, negotiations with Libya to renew collaboration on immigration issues are taking place. What Alfano's statement indicates is a possible route for *rescuing to deport:* Italy saves lives at sea and returns some people to the places they wanted to escape so badly that they risked their lives crossing the Mediterranean. Mare Nostrum is part and parcel of the ongoing re-organization of political interests in the Mediterranean that the Arab Uprisings forced in the region. Experts on marine search and rescue (SAR) operations, in fact, read Mare Nostrum's heavy-duty and hyper technological vehicles as more suited for terrestrial and border enforcement operations, rather than for delicate rescue operations and for assisting rescued people.

And it is in fact to the stories of some survivors that I now want to turn: stories of being ignored in the most heavily surveilled and trafficked sea in the world, stories of "shipwrecks with spectators," human eyes and technological eyes seeing boats in distress, *and* turning the other way, *and* not coming back with help – against the obligation to intervene sanctioned by maritime law. In March 2011,[19] a boat carrying Ethiopians and Eritreans fleeing the Libyan civil war[20] was "left-to-die"[21] while on the radar – both technically and symbolically – of many. When the boat started to take on water soon after leaving Tripoli, one of the passengers called an Eritrean priest in Rome who immediate-

---

http://www.terrelibere.org/4710-europa-fortezza-quanto-costano-i-progetti-sovrapposti.

[19] As I write, similar evidence is emerging about the shipwreck of October 11, 2013, which I reference in the opening. See the testimony by survivor Mohanad Jammo and the article by Fabrizio Gatti: 'Lampedusa: Passing the buck of responsibilities', *L'Espresso,* 28 novembre 2013. See also the video-interview with "Said," *Sorry for not drowning,* www.storiemigranti.org.

[20] Migrants living in Libya at the time of the Uprisings and the civil war.

[21] Heller, C, Pezzani, L., & Situ Studio (2012). *Forensic oceanography. Report on the "Left-to-die boat,"* available at: http://www.fidh.org/IMG/pdf/fo-report.pdf.

ly notified the Italian coastguard. With the phone information, the exact location of the boat was established and the highest emergency "Priority: Distress" was broadcast to all vessels (commercial, private, military) in the area. In parallel, the Italian coastguard also informed Malta authorities and NATO's headquarters. No help came.

But in the course of a fifteen-day tragedy, the passengers also encountered several of their non-rescuers: a military helicopter, launching down cookies and water and gesturing "we shall be back;" fishing boats; and a NATO amphibious warfare vessel with aircraft facilities onboard. This NATO vessel was so close, survivors recall, that they saw people on the deck taking photos of their sinking boat. Passengers held up the dead babies and empty fuel tanks in a last attempt to call for help.[22] Like all the other vehicles, however, the NATO vessel abandoned *sixty three* people to die – Libyan war refugees, the very same civilians the NATO boat was there to save as part of the "humanitarian military" intervention in the war in Libya. And, as one of the nine survivors explains, the 'humanitarian and military nexus' was part of the informed decision to leave, adding an even more chilling piece to this story of "military and humanitarian" non rescue:

> [when] the conflict started, the UN and Europeans [...] declared a no fly zone and NATO started bombing places around our area, we were scared. We hadn't planned to go to Italy before the war started but [...] we were afraid for our lives. *We knew that European and NATO ships and planes were patrolling the Mediterranean in force and it would be safer for us to go.*[23]

Epilogue

High-pitched emergency calls and the white noise of securitization are the powerful sound-scape of policy and public dis-

---

[22] Shenker, J. (2012, March 28). How a migrant boat was left adrift in the Mediterranean, *The Guardian*.
[23] Davis, S. (2012, October 28). *The left to die boat. A BBC Radio Documentary*, http://www.bbc.co.uk/programmes/p0101r27.

course about migration in Europe. In these pages, instead, I attended to the "noise in the waters" of migrant mobility, and worked toward a political articulation of humanitarian outcries against the marine cemetery in the Mediterranean. By 'political articulation' I mean a response that would not leave it to the natural element of water but that would engage with the multiple spaces, borders, and economies that criss-cross the Mediterranean; and a response that would not result in a Euro-med voice-over but that would give ear to the desires, the struggles, and the stories that migrate across the Middle Sea.

(November 2013; March 2014)

CONTRIBUTORS

GLENDA GARELLI is a Ph.D. candidate at the University of Illinois, Chicago where she works on a spatial inquiry of the European Union membership design, focusing on migration's contested spaces. At UIC she also teaches an undergraduate course on cinema and cities. Her research has been published in *Environment and Planning D: Society and Space, Postcolonial Studies, Materiali Foucaultiani*. She co-edited the book *Spaces in Migration* (Pavement Books, 2013) and is part of the editorial board of *Storie Migranti*, www.storiemigranti.org.

FRANCO NASI teaches Contemporary Italian Literature at the University of Modena and Reggio Emilia. He has written extensively on Romantic aesthetics, twentieth-cen-tury poetry and theater, and translation theory, and has translated American and English poets (Roger McGough and Billy Collins among others) into Italian. His most recent publications include *Specchi comunicanti* (Medusa 2010), *La maliconcia del traduttore* (Medusa 2008) and *I dilemmi del traduttore di Nonsense* (Longo 2012, edited with Angela Albanese).

THOMAS SIMPSON is Distinguished Senior Lecturer in Italian at Northwestern University. He has translated theater work by Marco Martinelli/Teatro delle Albe, Marco Baliani (with Nicoletta Marini-Maio and Ellen Nerenberg), Marco Paolini, Eduardo De Filippo, Pier Paolo Pasolini, Carlo Goldoni, Giorgio Strehler. In 2010 he published *Murder and Media in the New Rome*, a study of united Italy's first media circus.

www.ingramcontent.com/pod-product-compliance
Lightning Source LLC
Chambersburg PA
CBHW071222090426
42736CB00014B/2939